# Who's *in my* Mirror?

JUNE VOLGMAN (RISCHMAN)

*June Volgman*

WESTBOW
PRESS
A DIVISION OF THOMAS NELSON

*WestBow Press books may be ordered through booksellers or by contacting:*

*WestBow Press*
*A Division of Thomas Nelson*
*1663 Liberty Drive*
*Bloomington, IN 47403*
*www.westbowpress.com*
*1-(866) 928-1240*

*ISBN: 978-1-4497-5996-4 (sc)*
*ISBN: 978-1-4497-5997-1 (hc)*
*ISBN: 978-1-4497-5995-7 (e)*

*Library of Congress Control Number: 2012912601*

*Printed in the United States of America*

*WestBow Press rev. date: 08/09/2012*

# Acknowledgments

First I want to thank my very best friend, who instructed me to write this book and gave me the inspiration and direction. It has been an exciting and wonderful adventure. Thank you, Jesus.

My son Mark, who gave me the best advice, keep going until it is finished!

My niece Kristy, who gently showed me I needed to dig deeper and work harder.

My sister, Shirley, who assured me I could write.

My neighbor Barb always shared my excitement. She wants the first copy and is looking forward to reading it.

# Chapter One

Sue looked in the mirror and wondered, *where did that innocent little girl disappear to?* She had been an only child, doted over by two loving parents. She had felt so safe and secure. But was she? Twelve was such a tender age to lose so much. All these years later, those events played vividly in her mind, over and over again. She convinced herself no one had ever lived through anything like this.

*   *   *

Sue's husband, Dan, like most men, would rather know what is wrong and fix it than live helplessly on the outskirts of happiness. He repeatedly asked himself why he had been blind to all the warning signs and deaf to his friends' repeated advice: "Run for your life." After all these years of marriage, his love hadn't gone away, even though his wife kept rejecting it. He knew something was terribly wrong. When he tried to find out what it was, not only was the door slammed in his face, but she also lashed out like he was the one with a problem. Sometimes he wondered if it was time to walk out the door and never return. But could he really do that?

One of Dan's many days of escape found him sitting in his fishing boat. Anchored in his favorite spot, he watched as the bobber danced with each ripple but never disappeared under the water. He looked across the lake to where the water looked clear, peaceful, and inviting. But over the side of the boat, the water looked dark and mysterious. Like so many things, this reminded him of how he lived. Gazing from a distance, his wife looked beautiful and charming, with long auburn hair that fell gracefully around her face. It showed off her bright, beautiful blue eyes. But in reality she was also dark and mysterious.

Their story started in high school. Dan saw himself as just an ordinary guy, but many of the girls would have described him as tall, handsome, and having a great sense of humor. They loved his serious and romantic sides, the latter of which he did his best to hide. He didn't date much, but when he asked a girl out, he was never refused. That did a lot for his male ego. Everything changed when he met Sue. A few guys had asked her out, but she always had an excuse. Word spread fast, and it was, "Don't even bother; she will snap your ego like a rubber band, and it will sting."

\* \* \*

On a memorable April 1st. of Dan's junior year of high school, spring was in the air and pranksters were looking for unsuspecting victims. Dan had just finished his lunch and was on his way to his next class. He passed his friend Joe and asked: "Did your mom send something good to eat?" "She sure did and it's too bad you're going to miss out." Joe's mom loved to cook and bake. Around school she was known for the best cookies and donuts. Today Joe passed around her special homemade pizza. After his friends finished they all agreed it was the best pizza they ever ate. Joe stood up and in a somewhat loud voice said: "Now I am waiting for you guys to start barking." His friends looked at him quizzically and asked: "What are you talking about?" Joe answered: "April Fools! That was a dog food pizza!" His friends gagged and declared they were going to get him back, Big Time. Joe answered them, "This was my mom's idea, not mine. When my brothers and I were in grade school, we were more afraid of our mom's pranks than her discipline. One time she asked us if we wanted to go on a Gatton vacation. It took us only a few minutes to pack our bags and pile in the car. On the way we asked, "What is a Gatton vacation?" She answered, "It's a very special place your uncle Jim recently took his children and I thought you boys might enjoy going there." "Mom pulled into a gas station. After paying for the gas she headed straight to the car wash. As she started through, we quickly reached to roll-up our windows and the handles were gone. No one wanted to be called a sissy, so we all faced the water, the soap, the rinse, and finally the dryer that tried to erase our faces. When we pulled out she laughingly asked if we enjoyed our special vacation and told us we didn't have to shower that night. The next time we were naughty, we reminded our mom we were already punished."

\* \* \*

2

Dan was oblivious to how this day would totally change his future. When he turned the corner to go to his Spanish class, he bumped into Sue, and her books went flying. He picked them up for her, and she thanked him and walked away. After standing there a moment, his mind agreed with his eyes. *She is drop-dead gorgeous.* As he hurried to his next class, he reminded himself; t*hat girl doesn't date anyone.* The school year ended and he never saw her again. Not in the hallways or the lunch room. "Where did she disappear to?"

Dan wanted to get a job for the summer so he could save money to buy a car. A local grocery store hired him to stock shelves and bag groceries. He remembered that when he was little, his dad said to him, "Son, people always have to eat, so when you grow up, apply for jobs in the food industry." Dan was sure his dad didn't remember that, because now he wanted him to go to college and become a doctor, lawyer, or anything else that would produce wealth and greatness.

A week after he started his new job, Sue was hired there as a clerk. Dan didn't see her the first day because he was stocking shelves. On her second day, he was told to go bag for registers three and four. He tried to cover his surprise when he looked up and there she was. He had planned to use the summer as a time to totally forget her. Now that was not going to happen. By the end of the day, his distraction had brought many customer complaints. Tomatoes put on the bottom of a bag were squished. A caller claimed he put canned goods on top of bananas and they split. Dan's boss told him that was not acceptable and that his job was on the line. He knew he had to change. If he got fired, Dan would rather run away than face his dad and the never-ending lectures he'd have to listen to.

The evening before, Dan had rehearsed what to say to Sue. His plan was ready to go into action as he sat across from her in the break room. He asked, "How can you change a piece of chocolate into a vegetable?" Sue was curious and asked, "How?" "You toss it into the air and it comes down squash." Sue asked, "Is that your best joke?" "No, I have a better one. Why did the banana go out with the prune? Sue asked, "Why?" "It couldn't get a date." He noticed a grin on Sue's face as she got up and started walking away, so he got brave. "Sue would you go out on a "date" with me Friday night?" "No, I can't but thanks for asking." Dan found a ray of hope in her grin and her politeness. His senior year was approaching, and he thought it should be a time for students to start to act like adults and map out their life plans. Dan's map led right to Sue, and he needed a plan of action to get things moving. So he thought of funny things to say or do to make her laugh, and sometimes it worked. He also started using some of his paycheck to buy her gifts. And with such a small break room, it was easy to sit next to or across from her. Then one day, out of the clear blue, Sue started to not just listen but also to respond with interest. By the end of summer, even though she still refused to date him, he was sure things were moving in the right direction.

A week before school started their jobs ended and Dan was sure they would continue their friendship during the school year. The first day of school started, and they had no classes together. But Dan was positive he would run into her soon. That hope was dashed after a few weeks passed and he had not seen her anywhere. Dan had to admit to himself that she had probably changed schools or maybe her parents made a sudden decision to move.

Some of the guys kept telling him that Janet, a really popular girl in their class, had been trying to flirt with him and he was the only one who hadn't noticed. His friends encouraged him not to pass up the chance, but each time he talked to Janet, he felt as though he was cheating on Sue. After a while, though, he decided he would ask Janet for a date during Christmas break. He waited until the last day of school. They were sitting in the lunchroom together, and Dan was just about to ask her out when he felt someone looking at him. When he looked up, Sue was standing there. She paused, glared angrily, and walked away. Just then Janet asked Dan, "What was it you had to ask me about?" As he was getting up to go after Sue, he said to Janet, "Nothing. Just have a nice Christmas break."

He was so surprised to see Sue that when he caught up to her, he blurted out, "Will you marry me?" As she hurried away she glanced over her shoulder, and said nothing. He questioned himself, "Did I really just propose marriage, or do I think I did, but I actually didn't?" He let his mind linger on the look she had given him when she saw him talking to Janet. *No, there was no mistake; Sue was jealous and angry.* He smiled and had a renewed sense of hope.

Dan worked at the grocery store during Christmas break and hoped to see Sue return to work, but she didn't. When he and his family went to church on Christmas, he prayed never to see Sue again. Then he asked God to cancel that prayer. *I wonder if canceling a prayer is okay.* He stumbled around with his words because praying was something he knew very little about. Then he prayed a prayer he really meant: *God, can you somehow get Sue and me together? I really want to marry her someday! If you can't do that, would you help me forget her?* Then Dan told God he was giving him options and hoped he would do something.

\* \* \*

Sue arrived at home after Dan's proposal of marriage with mixed emotions. What she wanted and what she could have were two very different things. She could not afford the luxury of thinking about Dan. Sue's plan for the future consisted of having her picture taken and put on a deck of old maid cards. She started to cry at her own sick humor and then snapped herself back to reality. She could have a great career by saving for some kind of schooling. She thought she might want to become a flight attendant, as she would get to travel around the world and would never come back to this town.

\* \* \*

Dan's prayers and even his thoughts of Sue were temporarily pushed to the back of his mind. He had saved enough money to buy a car, and his dad promised to go with him to make sure he didn't end up with a lemon. His dad could wheel and deal with the best of them, and Dan was happy to have him along. The car his father picked out was an old man's car, not the souped-up, jamming chick magnet he dreamed about. But it really didn't matter, because it sure was better than his bike or borrowing his dad's car. *Anyway,* Dan reminded himself, *showing off really isn't my style.* With those kinds of thoughts, he was beginning to think like an adult. This was a good thing—especially if he was going to yell out any more marriage proposals.

Now with the responsibility of a car, Dan had to work every Saturday. His dad reluctantly gave in, but he also reminded him he needed good grades to go to college. Dan could not tell his father that all he wanted was to get a job at Great Foods Warehouse, marry his dream girl, and have a family.

One Saturday Dan was shocked to see Sue back at work. He was curious as to where she had been, but he decided not to ask. During lunch she shared with him her new dream of becoming an airline stewardess and said she was working to save money for schooling. Dan tried to share her excitement and even gave her a hug, but inside was yelling, "You can't do that; we are getting married."

When Sue arrived back home from work, she was mad at herself for telling Dan her goals and letting him hug her. Feelings were surfacing again that she had worked so hard to suppress. When she was younger, she would play house and her parents would join her. She had married prince charming, and her dolls were their three children. Her mom and dad would come and be their dinner guests. All those dreams were gone. Sometimes her sorrow would turn to anger toward God. "That could never have taken place if you were real. I never heard of this happening to anyone. What do you do, God? Think of new ways to hurt people and watch them suffer?" She cried herself to sleep, but when she awoke, the first thing on her mind was Dan. Sometimes no matter how hard people fight, they can't win. Sue could not love Dan, but she did.

Meanwhile, Dan was reliving what had happened. He had actually gotten to hug her. It was like he had climbed a mountain and was standing at the top. All that lack of oxygen put a wild idea in his head: he decided to pop the question. He used a bag of groceries. On a can of corn he wrote, "I am not being corny." On a jar of artichoke hearts: "I am all choked up, but I tell you I love you with all my heart." Written on a can of peas was, "Will you peas marry me?" He handed Sue the bag as they left work that evening. He had to make this some kind of joke; he knew he'd be turned down, but at least she would know how he felt.

On Monday, Dan was reminded of his foolishness. After his last class he went to his locker, and there was the bag. Giving the groceries back was Sue's polite way of saying no. He took the bag home to give to his mom. First he opened it to take the notes off, but to his surprise, it was not what he had given Sue. On a head of lettuce was written, "My mind won't leaf me alone about you." On a bunch of celery hearts was, "I have a heart for you." On a bottle of marjoram was, "Yes, I will marjoram you." After looking everything over again, there seemed to be no mistake about her answer. He realized two things. One was that they had never even dated, and another was that he had no ring. He was sure he was dreaming and that his mom would call him soon and wake him up for supper.

The next morning, that bag was still there as a reminder that he hadn't dreamed any of this. He decided to get an engagement ring and then go to school late. He spent his lunch hour looking for his bride-to-be, but she was nowhere to be found. All week, when he asked anyone if they'd seen her, their reply was "forget her." Saturday morning came, and Sue showed up at work. Dan waited until lunchtime and followed Sue to the break room. There he got down on one knee, opened the box, and proposed. Sue melted as she looked at the most beautiful and delicate ring she had ever seen. Just like that, they were planning a late June wedding. Sue insisted on eloping, and that was fine with Dan. He went right away to talk to his boss about Great Foods Warehouse and asked if he would be willing to put in a good word for him. He agreed, and Dan went back to tell Sue before they had to get back to work.

# Chapter Two

Years later, Dan was thirty-five years old and could see only a remnant of that seventeen-year-old boy. The image in the mirror kept fading, so he no longer asked it, "Who are you?" He felt that he needed help as much as his wife, even though he didn't know her problem. She seemed to be on an emotional roller coaster ride. His wife couldn't have any children, so it had been just the two of them—though not really. It felt to Dan as though Sue were living on an island, with a moat around it that couldn't be crossed by anyone, including him. He tried to swim through the strong current of her tears and the high waves of her pain, but he kept getting pushed back into the water. He felt he would someday cross over and be her Prince Charming. *Yes,* he thought, *even macho men sometimes believe in fairy tales.*

Dan had spent seventeen years working for Great Foods Warehouse. Many times they wanted to make him a foreman, but he always declined, not wanting to boss his friends around. One day at work he noticed a new guy who was filling orders with a smile on his face. Nobody else smiled while lifting all those heavy cases. So Dan figured it wouldn't be long until all that hard work would wipe his smile away. But it didn't. Finally, on break one day, Dan asked him. "Why are you smiling all the time?" Dan sure didn't expect what he heard next. He didn't even answer with a sentence; it was just one word: "Jesus!" That one word penetrated Dan like a bullet.

Dan pushed that event to the back of his mind, and day-to-day life just went on. One evening, he came home from work and there was a package for him on the table. His first thought was, *I didn't order anything. Sue wouldn't send me something; she would just hand it to me. It's not my birthday. Okay! Just open it.* To his surprise, it was a Bible. *Now who would send me a Bible and why?* He wondered. He set it on the table and forgot about it. A few nights later, he was in the den relaxing in his recliner when the Bible, which was just sitting there in front of him, seemed to call him. *How can this ordinary Bible call to me without actually saying anything?* He walked over and just looked at it. He reached to pick it up and then pulled his hand away. "Are you, a grown man, afraid of a book?" He answered himself with a yes and walked out of the room.

Weeks went by and Dan was back to feeling comfortable in his den. Then one evening he was leaning back in his recliner, reading his newspaper. He dozed off—or so it seemed. He saw the Bible open and was straining to read it, but he couldn't seem to get quite close enough. Then his eyes landed on Deuteronomy 4:29: "But if from thence thou shalt seek the Lord thy God, thou shalt find him, if thou seek him with all your heart and with all thy soul." Those words stayed with him; actually, it seemed as though they were haunting him. "Is this a game of hide-and-seek? Is God hiding somewhere? If he is, can he be found?" With the unanswered questions looming, he was glad when Sue called him for supper.

Sue said Dan looked pale and asked him if he felt okay. "I'm fine," was his response, but he was beginning to wonder about his condition. *After all,* he thought, *people that go crazy don't recognize what is happening.* Sue asked if he wanted to go shopping with her in the morning, and he declined by saying he had some things to look for.

"Anything I can help you with?" Sue asked.

"No I think he—I mean it's—hiding in the basement."

"It's not hiding, dear; you probably just misplaced it. All these years and you haven't learned to put things back in the same spot so you can find them when you want them."

*Okay God,* Dan thought, *I haven't even started, and already you got me a lecture from my wife.*

The following morning, after Sue left, Dan started walking around the house. "Hi, God, how are you? I am here looking for you." He got down on his knees and looked under the couch. "Hey, God, are you there? Come on; I am doing this seeking thing; how come I am not finding?" He then remembered he had told Sue he would be looking in the basement. As he walked down the stairs, he yelled, "God, I am coming! You weren't upstairs; you must be down here." He looked under his work bench, under the stairwell, and in cabinets, and he was still calling out to God.

Then he heard a voice behind him: "I'm here!"

He turned, but no one was there. It seemed to have come from the laundry room, so he looked in the washer and dryer. *Okay now what? Did*

*I imagine or was it real? If it was real, was it God? What would God be doing down in my basement?* He had found it kind of fun in a strange sort of way, but not anymore.

When Sue came home, he tried to act normal, but he wasn't quite sure what that was. Then the thought came to him, *what if there really is someone hiding out in our basement? If someone has access to my house, I have to protect my wife.* But if I call the police and no one is down there, everyone will think I'm going crazy. "Sue, what do you think about getting a dog?" he asked.

"You know what," she said, "I think that is a great idea!"

Dan grabbed his jacket and said, "Good, let's go!"

"You mean now?" she asked.

"Yes, no reason to wait."

So they headed to the humane society, and when they arrived, Dan had to contain himself so he wouldn't run to the door. He searched to find the biggest, meanest-looking dog. Sue was looking for a little, cuddly, gentle one. They were both pointing out different dogs. Finally Dan told her that he wanted her to be protected when he wasn't home. "But I am not afraid," she said.

"I know, but I will just feel better. Let's get this German Shepard. Nobody will ever bother you." That is what Dan said, but he was really thinking that whoever that voice in the basement belonged to wouldn't bother him anymore. While Sue was petting it and deciding, Dan was thinking, I *might be buying this big dog to protect me and my wife from God. Does that make sense? Yes! She doesn't even want to talk about church, so I sure can't tell her God might be living in our basement.* They paid for their new dog. The clerk that waited on us was a big, burly guy, and his name was George, so that became the dog's name. On the way home, they stopped at the pet store and bought everything they needed to take care of George and make him comfortable in his new home.

A couple of weeks later, after all the adjustments had been made and George had settled in, they decided he was a very good choice. Just when Dan was beginning to think everything was back to normal, something happened. He was sitting, reading his newspaper after supper as he usually did, with George lying at his feet. George got up, walked over to the table, picked up the Bible, and brought it back and set it on Dan's lap. Dan ignored what had just happened and kept reading his paper. Then George started whining. Dan picked the Bible up and said, "Okay, George, I will read to you." Dan questioned himself: "Are you really going to read the Bible to this dog that seems to be waiting and keeps staring? Well, it's either read or get the phone book, look up the number of a psychiatrist, and make an appointment for myself and for George."

After some hesitating and contemplating, Dan reluctantly picked the Bible up and put it in his lap. It fell open to the first chapter of Job. Dan asked George if he wanted to hear about Job, and he barked. Dan took that for a yes, but he guessed it might have been a no.

Dan began to read about this man, Job, who feared God. Dan wondered where Job had met him, because Dan didn't think they had basements back then. When Dan paused to ponder, George started to whine again. "Okay, okay, I will stick to the story. I will read it and break it down so you can understand it even if I can't."

Job seemed to be a pretty good guy, and God liked him. He was very wealthy and had a large family. George really liked the part about all the camels, sheep, and oxen. Job was observing his family and started to worry; he feared that they were getting wild and may have sinned. He made burnt offerings just in case. Meanwhile, the Lord was bragging about Job to a bunch of guys, including one named Satan. God sounded just like a parent that thinks his or her child is the best. Satan responded by saying, "Sure he loves you, but that is because you give him everything; he is a spoiled brat. If you took it all away, he would curse you to your face." It seemed that this serpent was accusing God of buying Job's friendship by giving him things. God responded by saying, "All that he hath is in thy power, only upon himself put not forth thine hand." It seemed God was insisting that he didn't force anyone and that Satan couldn't force anyone either. Instead of continuing to trust God, Job listened to Satan, and the more he listened, the more afraid he became. That had a snowball effect. The more fear set in, the more he lost. Then Job decided that the Lord giveth and the Lord taketh away.

George never budged through all the pages of accusations and of Job's life getting worse and worse. When Dan started chapter 38, George perked up like he was now getting to the good part. How did he know? The Lord answered Job out of a whirlwind, and said, "Who is this that darkeneth counsel by words without knowledge? Gird up thy loins like a man, for I will demand of thee, and answer thou me."

George, said Dan, "This Job guy got himself into lots of trouble and now has to answer to God. Movies and books usually have happy endings; is there one here?"

Dan sat and thought about what he had read so far, and it sure was making him feel uneasy and wanting to hide. *But if God were living here,* he thought, *where could I go?* Dan was taking a bit too long, and George started whining again. As soon as Dan started reading, again, he was shocked! Job was sorry for all the things he had said against God, and he repented in dust and ashes. Then God spoke to Job's friends and told them they hadn't spoken of the thing that is right, as his servant Job had. "Did you hear that, George?" Dan said. "After Job repented, he became the good guy, just as though he never sinned. All of his friends were still in trouble. God instructed them to go to Job with repentance; and they did, and Job forgave them. When God saw Job being forgiving, he gave him twice as much as he had had before.

Job's family arrived, and they ate and comforted him over all the evil that the Lord had brought upon him, and they gave him money and gold. "This is a little confusing, George. Why would people bring Job money and gold when Job had been the richest man of the east and now was twice as rich as before? What kind of comfort do you bring someone that God is blessing? Let's do some detective work here. If God did this evil to Job, why would Job have to repent of his accusations? Why would Job have to forgive his friends if they were speaking the truth about God? Hmm."

Dan closed the book and petted George and said, "Did you get something out of this? Now, it's okay if this helps me be nicer, but I don't want that to happen to you. You're the big, bad guard dog here, especially if that voice in the basement comes back. After all this reading, I don't know what to think about God or if I would even want him in my house." Then Dan thought about Stan at work and all the smiling he did because he had Jesus. "I guess sometime I will just have to read some more. I want to know if God is good, evil, or both. Opinions are abounding so far."

The following weekend Dan and Sue were out walking George, and Dan said, "Do you think we could go to church sometime?"

She answered back, "Why?"

Dan couldn't come up with an answer, so there was just silence until they saw some friends coming their way walking their dog. The two couples stopped to talk and watch the dogs greet each other. The other couple's dog was a little intimidated by George, and Dan was glad to see that. After returning to their walk, Dan hoped the conversation would come back to going to church, but it didn't.

That night, while lying in bed, Dan started thinking about recent events and what he should do. After Sue's response, or non-response, when Dan asked her about going to church, Dan figured he had better not share with her any of the strange things that had been happening. *She lives a life that is separate from ours, and now I am forced to do the same to her. It's not like I am cheating on her. I just want to find out about God—if he is real, what he is like, and whether he lives in our basement. I guess I have to keep George's secret too. How would Sue take it if I told her we seem to have a dog that is interested in the Bible? I just can't risk it. She might throw us both out.*

# Chapter Three

Life for Sue could not be changed. She spent many sleepless nights trying to think of a solution or at least something to ease the pain. The thought of counseling and vocalizing what had happened to her was something she could not bring herself to go through. Besides, no one could make it go away, and some might not even believe her.

Dan brought Sue some happiness, but she was sure she could never bring him any. Why he had stayed around all these years, she didn't know. When she first met Dan, she was not looking for a boyfriend. Sue tried everything she could think of not to like him. She remembered the day she bumped into Dan on the way to class and books went flying. But that wasn't all. Inside her, sparks were flying like it was the Fourth of July. Finding out Dan's class schedule was not easy, but it was the only way she could avoid him. She really thought that would work. She also thought she could get a part-time job and just forget him, but that sure backfired.

Once, Dan even wrote a list of things about himself that he would be willing to change just for Sue. She knew that meant he was getting way too serious—and that she was too, no matter how hard she tried to deny it. Finally, when he proposed, there was no way Sue could stop herself from saying yes. As soon as they married, she knew it was a mistake. How could someone so miserable bring happiness to someone else?

Sue knew there was something going on with her husband, but she didn't know what. She almost hoped he was having an affair and would soon ask for a divorce. Maybe all that time he claimed to be in the den, he was sneaking out the window to meet someone and get back before it was time to go to bed. Then she would get angry at the thought that he might do such a thing.

*   *   *

Meanwhile, Dan was trying to deal with all the changes in his life, none of which was anything like what his wife was thinking about. There wasn't another woman; it was a dog that kept bringing him a Bible to read. Add to that a voice in the basement and a guy at work that talked like Jesus was his best friend. What next?

One day Dan was driving home from work, thinking about his fishing trip with his neighbor and what bait to use to entice and catch some beautiful bass. Then he heard, "My love is my bait." Dan looked in his rearview mirror and glanced in the backseat but didn't see anyone. He pulled over to the side of the road. He looked around, not expecting to see anyone—and he didn't. He also couldn't explain what he had heard. The voice was loud, yet not audible, but it was very real. After a time of contemplation, he made his decision. It was showdown time—tonight!

That evening Sue left to go to the movies with a friend. Dan wondered if God set that up. *Maybe he wants a showdown too.* Dan watched out the window, and as soon as Sue was out of sight, he marched into the den, picked up the Bible, and declared, "Whoever you are that talks to people without being seen, uses love for bait, and gets animals to do things that are most unusual, we are going to have it out, right here and now! If you want to tell me something in this Bible, what is it? I refuse to read the whole thing. If this is just some kind of joke, it is not funny. Well, maybe it is for you, but it isn't for me."

Dan wasn't doing too well having it out with God, so he sat down, and right away George went and got the Bible and set it on his lap. He decided to just start at the beginning: Genesis 1. It didn't take long for him to realize that when God spoke, something happened. "Check this out, George. On the fifth day, the waters brought forth moving creatures—which would be fish for me to catch. The next day, he created your ancestors, the beasts of the earth, after his kind.

"After creating man, God decided man needed a helpmate. The Lord God caused a deep sleep to fall upon Adam. He took one of Adam's ribs and closed up the flesh. The rib, which the Lord God had taken from the man Adam, made a woman, and he brought her unto Adam. God gave them instructions to run the garden they were in."

"Listen to this, George, now we have a talking serpent. He was more subtle than any beast of the field, and he asked the woman, 'Yea, hath God said ye shall not eat of every tree of the garden?' She answered the serpent: 'We may eat of the fruit of the trees of the garden: But of the fruit of the tree which is in the midst of the garden, God hath said, Ye shall not eat of it, neither shall ye touch it, lest ye die.' This must be the first lie, because God never told her she would die if she touched it. Then the serpent called God a liar and said to her, 'Ye shall not surely die. For God knows that in the day ye eat thereof, then your eyes shall be opened, and ye shall be as gods, knowing good and evil.' What kind of offer was that? If they had everything good, why would they want to know evil? What attraction is there to evil, and why?

"The plot thickens. God came to confront them, but they hid themselves from his presence. The Lord God called unto Adam and said unto him, 'Where art thou?' He said, 'I heard thy voice in the garden, and I was afraid, because I was naked; and I hid myself.' Then God got on their case and asked them, 'Who told thee that thou wast naked?' Listening to the serpent caused them to run from God and get in a lot of trouble.

"Uh oh! Things are getting worse. It looks like when God confronted them, they both passed the buck. Eve said, 'The serpent beguiled me, and I did eat.' Adam told God that the woman he gave him had handed him the fruit to eat. Neither one said they were sorry. I think they set a pattern that is still the same. Some people enjoy evil, run from God, and like to pass the buck."

During lunch break the following day, Dan wanted to tell Stan what he was reading, but it never seemed to be the right time. After work, he rushed home and told Sue he wasn't hungry and went into the den. George was right behind him but didn't warn him that Sue was also behind him. Dan caught a glimpse of her out of the corner of his eye just when he was about to pick up the Bible. He turned and said, "Maybe I am hungry, what's for supper?"

She answered, saying, "Pork chops baked in milk, mashed potatoes, and green beans."

"You know, that sounds so good, I am suddenly very hungry."

As he followed her to the kitchen, he thought, *that was a close call. What will I ever say if she catches me? I will pass the buck like Adam and Eve did and explain it was our dog's idea, not mine.*

The next evening Dan was smarter. He waited to see what Sue was going to do after supper. She decided to go through her coupons and sort and cut out the good ones. He knew that gave him at the very least an hour. He went into the den, grabbed the Bible, and opened it to where he had left off. In that hour, he and George learned a lot. In Genesis 6, mankind had become totally evil. "I don't think I ever met anyone who's every thought, every word, and everything they did was evil. Each and every human was corrupt except Noah, who found grace in God's sight. Noah obeyed God and built an ark. Then the earth was flooded to clean up all the evil. Afterward it didn't take Noah long to mess up. "I don't know if I am reading this right, but Noah gets drunk, undresses, and passes out. Ham comes in and sees his naked dad and performs what might be the first recorded homosexual and incest act. The other two sons come in backward to cover their dad and keep themselves from temptation. Ham brought a curse on his family, and the other two sons brought blessings on theirs." As Dan was putting the Bible down, Sue walked in. She glanced at the table but didn't say anything. They walked the dog, had a snack, and went to bed.

Dan woke up in the morning and was happy to be leaving on a fishing trip with his neighbor. He told himself today was all about fish and how to outsmart them. They weren't anchored and set up for more than five minutes before Dan had a fight on his hands. It was a beautiful five-pound, two-ounce bass. Right away Tom had his chance, and he landed one just a little bigger. After a few minutes of quiet, Dan asked him if he had ever read the Bible. His response was, "A long time ago I took a Bible class, and there is quite a bit about fishing. I even think Jesus prepared a fish dinner once." Dan hadn't read anything like that yet, so he asked if Tom knew where it was. He wasn't sure, but he thought it was in the red-letter part. The bending of their poles ended their fishy conversation. They each caught four more nice fish, which was their limit. They couldn't wait to get back home, clean them, and put them on the grill. As they were headed back to shore, Dan said, "I have one more question. Do you think Jesus put his fish recipe in the Bible?" Tom didn't know.

When Dan and Tom arrived back home, they found their wives had everything else ready, so they got the grill going and cleaned their fish, and within a short time they were sitting down to a very fresh fish dinner. Tom asked the girls if they had had a backup plan in case he and Dan returned empty-handed. They both shook their heads. That was a great shot for their male egos. But it didn't last long; the women ganged up against them and won three games of cribbage.

\* \* \*

Early Sunday morning Dan woke up suddenly and jumped out of bed. Sue wouldn't be up for at least a couple of hours. He quietly got dressed and went out to his car. As he backed out of the driveway, he asked himself, "Where are you going?" He shrugged his shoulders and just started driving until he spotted a church. He pulled up in front and stopped. *Okay, what do I have to lose?* He asked. "God, what do you think of this one?" he waited and waited, and nothing happened. He went to five others and did the same thing, but he received no answer. *Maybe God isn't here. He could still be at home in my basement, because I forgot to invite him along.* "Are you mad at me, God? I sure am sorry if I did something wrong."

Dan made it back home, went into the kitchen, and started breakfast. Sue came in and said, "I was awakened by this wonderful aroma. What's up? It's not my birthday. Should I be suspicious? Are you hiding something from me?"

"I am guilty; I just want to make my wife happy." Sue complimented my cooking and then asked if I minded if she went over to the neighbors' to help design invitations for their daughter's wedding. I said yes so fast that it was like pushing her out the door in her pajamas. I couldn't help it; I felt as though I had an appointment.

When she finally left, I headed to the den, picked up my Bible, and opened it to the book of Matthew. George looked sad because I wasn't reading out loud, so I told him I couldn't pronounce any of the names. Then, in the eighteenth verse, it started telling about the birth of Jesus. In verse 21, it explained that his name would be Jesus and that he would save his people from their sins. To Dan, that sounded like a heavy load.

Next Dan told George to close his ears because he wasn't going to like what he was reading about. "This guy named John shows up, whose clothes were made of camel hair and cowhide. His diet was locusts and honey. Protein and energy, I'll pass! People came and repented, and John baptized them and said, 'I indeed baptize you with water unto repentance: but he that cometh after me is mightier than I, whose shoes I am not worthy to bear: he shall baptize you with the Holy Ghost, and with fire.' I like a fire in the fireplace, but not on me." Sue walked in the door just when Dan was telling George that was enough until later.

"What are we having for lunch?" Dan asked.

"What would you like, dear?"

"Oh, maybe some locusts and honey—I mean, a roast beef sandwich and soup"

"Was there something else you wanted?"

"No."

"I thought you said something before roast beef."

"I think soup and a sandwich is plenty; do you want some help?"

"No dear, I think you should go rest. Is work getting to you?"

"No, but I am going to the den to relax a few minutes."

Dan picked up the Bible and started talking to it. "You have me questioning my sanity, and now I think my wife might be too. I heard people say they found comfort in reading the Bible, but it is causing a great disturbance in me."

Dan was happy to get back to work on Monday, except that Stan kept glancing his way. Dan was thinking, what's the big deal? Stan asked, "How was your weekend? Do anything interesting?" Out of Dan's mouth came, "I had locust and hon—I mean . . . a great roast beef sandwich." Stan turned his head, and Dan got a glimpse of a grin on his face. *Was he smiling because the only thing I could think of to say was a roast beef sandwich, or does he know something? God wouldn't tell him what is going on in my house; there is some privacy law that protects us. God could get in big trouble. But how would I file a complaint against him? And then would I send the police to my basement to arrest him? Sue would probably have me committed, and I would get in trouble with God. I think I will just keep my mouth shut.*

The rest of the week was uneventful. Dan worked, came home, enjoyed time with Sue, cleaned out the garage, watched TV, and stayed out of the den. By the weekend he was champing at the bit. It was like he had gone to a movie and during intermission was just waiting to find out what would happen next. After breakfast he headed to the basement and was casually cleaning his workbench. He didn't get much done because he kept glancing around, hoping to hear or see something. Tears started to well up in his eyes. He was missing the voice! He told himself that men don't do stuff like this, and he ran upstairs and into the den and closed the door. Right away there was a whimpering, and when he let George in, it almost looked like there were tears in his eyes as well.

Dan didn't care that Sue was home and might catch him. He grabbed the Bible and sat down, and it fell open. His eyes were fixed on 1 Samuel 3:4, and he read there that the Lord called Daniel, who answered by saying, "Here I am." Dan reread the passage and saw that it said the Lord called Samuel. He was sure the first time he read it he saw his name. He backed up to the beginning and found that this Samuel was just a child who ministered to the Lord before Eli. Samuel fell asleep, and when the call came from the Lord, Samuel thought it was Eli, so he ran to Eli and said "Here I am." This happened again and again. Samuel did not yet know the Lord. "Here it is again, George; it looks like a person can know the Lord, and he does talk to people. Eli told Samuel to go lie down: "And it shall be, if he calls thee, that thou shalt say, 'speak Lord, for thy servant heareth.' So Samuel went and lay down in his place, and the Lord spoke to him."

The weekend arrived, and Dan had fishing on his mind. It looked like a perfect day for the bass to have a big appetite. There was a little breeze from the west. The saying goes, "Wind from the east, fishing is least; wind from the west, fishing is best." Dan knew he had better get some things done first. He vacuumed and washed both of his vehicles. *Now I had better get the grass cut before Sue says, "Dan, the grass is sure getting tall." She never gives me orders, but she gives me big subtle hints with a little sweetness in her voice.*

Just as Tom and Dan finished packing up and were ready to go fishing, clouds rolled in and it started to rain. They left anyway because there was no lightning. By the time they got to the lake, it was raining hard enough to stir up the waters, making for upset fish that don't bite. As we sat in the boat getting soaked without a sign of any hungry fish, Tom decided they should just give up. Dan said, "As long as we're here, let's just give it another half an hour." He started to quietly talk to Jesus, one fisherman to another, and told him their wives were making everything else and just waiting for them to bring the fish. Then he asked if Jesus could help them. Tom was going to reel in and pack up, but Dan said to him, "Don't do that; I think some fish are coming our way."

After the half hour had gone by, Dan's pole bent just as he went to grab it, and he had a battle on his hands. He worked that fish, talked to it, talked to Jesus, talked to Tom, and talked to himself. Tom tried to get him to calm down, saying that it was just a fish. Dan thought to himself, *No, this is not just a fish; this is one supplied by Jesus.* When Tom netted it, they were both surprised at the size and figured it was plenty for all four of them. Just then Tom's pole bent, and *he* had a fight on his hands. When Dan netted and weighed it, he found it was just slightly smaller than the other. Tom said, "Time to go home, show off our fish, and start up the grill. When Dan was backing up the truck to hitch up the boat, it stopped raining, the sun came out, and a rainbow appeared. Dan stopped and said,

"Jesus, I think you might have had something to do with this, and I thank you if you did."

Tom's and Dan's wives were not nearly as surprised as Tom and Dan that they had brought home fish. Even though the fish were huge, they still tasted good. The girls said they didn't taste fishy at all. I had to ask what they meant by that. "Aren't fish suppose too taste fishy?" I asked. "Does that mean corn shouldn't taste corny? How about ham shouldn't taste hammy?" Dan got strange looks, even from Tom. "Okay, Okay, I will can the uncanny jokes." They started to laugh, and it was Dan's turn to give them strange looks.

On the way out the door the following morning, Dan passed the den, backed up, went in and picked up the Bible, and left. On the way to work, he asked himself, "Why did you bring this Bible?" He answered himself: "Because I don't think I can wait until tonight to find out more about Jesus—I mean, if Jesus prepared the fish he caught."

"Do you know you will get ribbed from the guys at work if you walk in with this book?"

"Yes I do, and I am wondering why. There are billions and billions of books that have been written, and yet this seems to be the only one that disturbs people and causes ridicule. Why is that?"

"I don't know, but I sure am curious why I have to debate with myself as to whether I will carry it into work or not. Do I want to risk this? It's almost like my manhood is on the line."

The only thing Dan took into work was his lunch bucket.

# Chapter Four

That evening Sue left to go to her knitting club. Two of the women who had recently invited Jesus into their life found everything going much better. They wanted to help Sue with her unknown problem, so they suggested a Bible study. Sue couldn't get out of there fast enough. If God hadn't been there for her when she needed him, she sure didn't want him now; it was too late. She rushed home, just wanting to see her husband and forget what had just happened. She walked in and saw the den door was closed. She quietly opened it and didn't like what she saw. Dan was reading the Bible, and it looked like George was listening. They were so focused they didn't even notice her. She shook her head and quietly closed the door. *What's with this Bible stuff all of a sudden?* She thought.

Sunny days bring people to gardening and other outdoor activities. But for many women, including Sue, their favorite thing to do is shop. *My neighbor's daughter is getting married, and that calls for a new dress*, Sue thought. On her way she turned a corner and saw a Christian bookstore. *It must be new.* Without thinking about it, she pulled in and parked. Inside was an unbelievable sight; there were so many books: hundreds—no, thousands—written about God. Upon inquiring as to how long the store had been here, Sue was shocked to hear "ten years." She was amazed to see all the different subjects, including faith, obedience, marriage, children, and prophecy. By far the biggest section was on love. *Okay, I am even more confused. How could an uncaring God have such a large selection on love?* Then there was the Bible section, with so many to choose from and some very expensive. Sue settled on a New Testament that didn't cost much. *I don't need the whole Bible to prove what God is like. But once I do, I will show Dan and those women in my knitting circle that they are just wasting their time.*

Sue felt relieved to be out of that store and on the way to buy a dress. She found two that she really liked, but she couldn't make up her mind and just purchased both. *One for the wedding and one for? Dan and I don't do much that requires dressing up, so I guess I will figure it out later.* Once home, she hid the Bible in her sock drawer. She went into the kitchen to make lunch and thought, *Why am I hiding a Bible? Maybe for the same reason Dan is hiding his Bible reading from me. I just don't know what that reason is.* She headed back to her bedroom, opened it, closed it, and put it back. *Forget it, my stomach says lunchtime.* Afterward she went outside to work in her garden. When she finished weeding and watering, she looked around and saw that it was beautiful. She looked up at the sky, and the blue was the prettiest she had ever seen. She thought someone nice had to have done that. While she was looking, she spoke to God for what she thought was the first time. "If you did all this, then you can't be all evil. But if you are good at all, how could such a horrible thing happen to me?" She paused and then addressed herself: "Stop it, Sue; just go in the house and start supper."

Sue had just finished preparing the meal when Dan came home, and after they ate, he helped her clean up and then headed for the den. Sue took out some cookbooks to look up some new recipes. She felt she was in a rut, preparing the same meals over and over again. *Expanding my horizons will take us around the world in meals,* she thought.

After getting as far as China and picking out a couple of dishes, it was time for Sue to check up on her husband. She walked down the hall, hoping he wasn't reading the Bible—but he was. She quietly closed the door and went back into the kitchen to her cookbook adventure, but she couldn't concentrate. She had all sorts of unanswered questions with no logical explanations. So she scurried to the bedroom, snatched up her Bible, went into her sewing room, and closed the door. She turned the chair around so that if Dan walked in, he wouldn't see that she was doing and hiding the same thing he was doing.

*Do I open it randomly or start from the beginning?* Sue wondered. She closed her eyes, opened it, and pointed. She looked down and saw 1 Thessalonians 5:9, which read, "For God hath not appointed us to wrath, but to obtain salvation by our Lord Jesus Christ." *What does that mean? Good, I have a dictionary right here. "Appoint" means "to assign, designate, allot." "Wrath" means "an angry act, one of punishment." So God doesn't point a finger and say, "Okay, it is your turn to hurt." But then why do I feel like I have had so much pain and punishment?*

23

June Volgman (Rischman)

At bedtime, Sue's mind was going a mile a minute. It started to wander to where she didn't want it to go, so she needed to think about something else. She looked for a little humor and found it: *My husband and I are playing a little cat-and-mouse game. If we don't make specific plans, we sneak in separate rooms to read the Bible.*

# Chapter Five

The drive to work in the morning was a good time for Dan to think about where this was all going and whether he would ever find any answers. Stan was a really nice guy, but didn't volunteer the information he needed. How do you ask a person to tell you about someone that died hundreds, maybe thousands of years ago?

Break finally came, and Dan rushed to sit in the chair across from Stan. Stan looked up and smiled, and then he opened his Bible and began to read. Dan sat there staring, waiting for him to share something or maybe show an expression of some kind to give him a clue. Just then Stan started to chuckle, and Dan strained his eyes to see where he was reading, but with the Bible being upside down and small print, he couldn't make it out. Then Stan suddenly began laughing out loud, and Dan wanted to yell at him, "What's so funny!" He restrained himself, but he didn't know if he could take one more laugh. Then he started to get mad. *If he doesn't want to talk to me, he should tell me to get lost. Usually when people start laughing they are willing to share so someone else can laugh too. He doesn't drive me to drink, but he is driving me to open that Bible tonight to try to find out what's so funny. I want to laugh too, and share it with George.* The work bell rang, and Dan had to cool down and get back to his job. I wouldn't even look at Stan, because I didn't want him to see my anger.

When Dan arrived at home, there was a wonderful meal already dished out. That usually meant Sue was either going somewhere or had some kind of project to work on right after supper. She announced she had a little shopping to do and wouldn't be gone long. Dan walked into the den to find George waiting for him. He picked up his Bible and spoke to George. "We are going to look for two things. Number one, something hilarious; and secondly, Jesus preparing a fish dinner. He finished Matthew without finding anything he was looking for. Instead, he found it very sad. It seemed like the more good things Jesus did, the madder people got.

Dan heard Sue walk in the door, and a short time later he heard the phone ring. He started reading again but was curious to find out who had called. He walked down the hall to Sue's sewing room, but she wasn't there. Turning to go check the kitchen, he caught something out of the corner of his eye and looked, and then he did a double-take. There was no doubt about it; there on her table laid an open Bible. He hurried back to the den and closed the door. He looked at George and said, "You will not believe what I just saw. You would not guess it in a million years. It's so unbelievable I can hardly say it. George, Sue is reading a Bible just like you and I are. The few times I brought up God, or maybe going to church, she either clammed up or changed the subject. George, we have to keep this a secret. She might get upset if she knew we knew. That's also why she can't know we are doing the same thing. She might quit and want us to quit. George, this is a fine mess you have gotten us into. You're a sneak and have made me one. I am passing the buck like Adam did. God, it's that dog you gave me."

"In studying some more, it looks like God and Jesus are both so loving and kind, and they offer many blessings. Then it looks like they're punishing and hurting people. I sure wouldn't want to make friends with someone who would help me out, give me gifts, and then knock me out and steal my wallet. Maybe that's why you don't see a lot of people carrying around and reading Bibles—they're confused too and just don't want to bother. I guess what is different for me is that happy, happy Stan! He's reading the Bible all the time, and he is the happiest guy I know! Besides, he is nice to people and helps when he can. But best of all, he doesn't belt me one for every break and lunch hour I just sit across from him, watching him read the Bible.

"The end of Luke, and finally I get to fish. In 24:41, Jesus asked for meat. They gave him a piece of broiled fish and honeycomb, and he ate it before them. I sure was hoping to find more on fish than that. Like maybe a recipe or two. What I am finding is a lot of fishing for men, which seems to be done by preaching or teaching the Bible, with some miracles in the mix. So is God fishing for me, and is the Bible—and maybe even Stan—the bait? If that's the case, I am going to keep taking the bait and see what, if anything, God is going to do. I have too much time invested in this to quit now. Besides, part of reading a book is the ending."

Dan didn't hear Sue go back to her sewing room, but it was not like her to be on the phone that long. Dan wondered if she had told anyone she was reading the Bible. *Probably not,* he thought. *I can't remember the last time she talked to her mom; and I think I am her closest friend, and she sure is not going to tell me.*

"Ah ha! Here is a man like me. He came to Jesus by night and concluded Jesus couldn't do any of these miracles unless God was with him. Jesus answered, saying, 'Except a man be born again, he cannot see the kingdom of God.' Nicodemus is thinking the same way I would. 'How can a man be born when he is old? Can he enter the second time into his mother's womb, and be born?' So Jesus told him that unless a man is born of water and of the Spirit, he cannot enter into the kingdom of God. It looks like he is trying to get some kind of commitment. I am going down in the basement to tell him just how I feel.

"Hey God, are you down here? I really want to talk to you. If you really do love me, I do want you in my life. But if you are going to beat me up and make me suffer, I honestly don't need or want that. I already have my fill. I know you talk, so would you please let me know before I make a decision? The Bible has a lot of good things and a lot of bad things. Are you doing them all? Do you have a split personality?"

Dan waited and waited, and there was no answer. "Okay, God, I'm not going to rush you. I'll stay down here because I really need information. So he sat and paced and looked around, and he talked and listened: Nothing, nothing, nothing. *Now what?* He thought. *Should I just give up?* "Can't you just tell me if you love me or not? It's just a yes-or-no question. Please." He waited some more—still no answer.

Finally he gave up and started up the stairs. Just then he heard "I'm here."

He ran back down the stairs and yelled "Where? Where are you? Don't you remember those were the first two words you spoke to me when we started this game of hide-and-seek? I want to keep going forward, not backward. What about all my questions?" *Unless this isn't God and someone is playing a very bad practical joke on me and right about now is laughing very hard listening to me babble on and on to God.*

Just then Sue called from the top of the stairs: "Dan, you have a phone call."

Dan thought that perhaps God was being more conventional and was calling him on the phone to talk and give him some answers. On the way up he asked Sue if she knew who was calling. She said she didn't recognize the voice. *Maybe it really is him, Dan thought.* It wasn't; it was a cousin of his neighbors. He was visiting from out of state and wanted to know where the best bass fishing was and the best lures to use that time of the year. After Dan gave him some ideas, he wished him good luck and hung up. *Right now I feel like a fish that has been outsmarted by God. The problem is, he won't reel me in and he won't let me go. He's probably just having fun laughing at me. I've been searching to find God's humor, but I never thought I would be the object of it.*

Dan was done with God for the moment and wanted to spend some time with his wife. So they took George for a walk. Dan maneuvered them past a church in the neighborhood to see if Sue would say something, but she didn't. Neither of them spoke. *We are both having Bible affairs behind the other one's back. I sure hope hers is going better than mine. I keep feeling like giving up, but I just can't.*

The alarm went off, and it seemed to Dan that he had just gone to bed. His plan for the day was the same as it seemed to be every day—get some answers! At work Dan waited for lunch to sit across from Stan and hoped he would say something to him. He wanted to ask Stan if God ever talked to him and if it was more than a few words. As usual, he was silent. *Between him and God, I don't know which is worse. I don't mean worse worse; I just mean more frustrating. I would like to get them both in the same room and use that big, hot light they use above people in movies to get them to talk. I can see it now. They are sitting at the table with that hot light in their faces, expressionless, and I'd say . . . well, smarty, what would you say? Okay, I would start out with "I want the facts, nothing but the facts." Could I say "so help you God" to God?* Just then lunch ended and everyone returned to work.

When Dan left work that evening, he walked out with Stan, and just as Dan was getting into his truck, Stan said, "Would you like to go to church with me sometime?"

"Yes," said Dan

"Good," said Stan, and he got in his car and drove away. He didn't stop to talk about the details, like when and where; he just left. Dan did, however, catch a big grin on his face as he drove by.

After Dan and Sue had supper together, it was another night of secrets with no end in sight. Dan watched as Sue walked into her sewing room and closed the door. George followed him to the den. *I don't know if I tell better stories or if it's just that we males have to stick together,* Dan thought. Before starting, Dan wondered if Sue knew what he was doing, like he knew what she was doing but didn't want to say anything. *If she does, we are both good at keeping secrets. They always have a way of coming out, but this is one I don't think will hurt anyone.*

Dan got back to the book of John, and seeing what he had to say about God. *This is kind of like working a puzzle. I keep looking for enough pieces to get a clear picture of what I want to know. Does God love me? If he does, is it right now, or is it a pie-in-the-sky kind of love that appears after we die?* Listen to this, George: "God is a spirit and they that worship him must worship him in spirit and in truth." So if spirits can go through walls that would be how God got in my basement. Maybe he didn't talk to me because I didn't worship him.

Friday at work, Stan didn't say anything about going to church, so Dan asked him. He wrote down his phone number, times of service and noted that Dan should just give him a call when he wanted to go. That was easy—no pressure, no commitment—which was good, because Dan was not going to lie to Sue to go to church. But Stan hadn't given Dan the name and address, so he couldn't go without calling Stan first.

As had been planned that evening, Sue and Dan went for a fish fry. While waiting for their order, Dan said, "You seem to be off in a distance somewhere" "Yes, there have been some unusual things that occupy my mind lately." "Could you expand and explain what you mean?" "All I can tell you is, if I could I would, but I can't." Dan said, "I am always ready to listen, whatever it is." He squeezed her hand and smiled. The waitress came with their order, and they enjoyed their fish. In between bites, Dan tried to pump Sue about Sunday morning, but he couldn't seem to get her to commit to anything. Not even a shopping trip seemed to spark her interest.

# Chapter Six

As Sue watched Dan leave for fishing early Saturday morning, she said, "Good riddance! I really don't mean that, George, but we have things to do. First I will take you for your morning walk." Sue tried to pump George for information about where he and Dan were in the Bible, and if they were learning anything. Sue threatened not to give him breakfast, but he didn't break. "Okay, George, if you're going to keep your mouth shut for Dan, then you better keep quiet for me. As soon as we get back home, I am going church hunting. Yes, I will feed you first."

Sue backed down the driveway without knowing where she was going. "Okay God, which direction?" She paused. "No answer. So on to plan B. Eenie, meenie, miney, moe, which way do you want me to go? I choose this very best one, so I am headed south."

At each church Sue found, she did the same thing. When she pulled into the parking lot, she made an inquiry to God. When she didn't get an answer, she wrote down the name, address, and times of services. After about ten stops, she found one called "Love in Jesus Fellowship." *That sounds good. It seems to say that we should love Jesus, but also that we will find love in Jesus. Mission accomplished. Now I can go home and try to figure out how to get here without Dan knowing.*

When Sue got back, she was excited, but now she had a dilemma. *How do I get there? I sure don't want to tell a lie so I can go and hopefully find out some truth. I could just walk out the door with my knitting bag and say I will be back in time to make lunch. I could tell him I am going shopping and then go to church and stop on the way home. But what if Dan asks questions just during a conversation?* "Okay God," she finally said, "how about this: if you want me to go to church, you figure out how I am going to get there without lying to my husband."

*Dan won't be home for a few hours yet so what should I do? Clean the house, work in the garden, knit, or go in my sewing room and read the Bible? If I am going to make it to church soon, I better take this opportunity to read the Bible while he is gone.* George followed Sue into the sewing room and sat at Sue's feet just like he did with Dan.

Sue had already read all of Matthew and Mark. She finished Luke and John as well, and they were all about Jesus. Some of the things he said and did were kind of hard for her to understand. It seemed to her that the Bible was in English and in code at the same time. Just when something looked clear to her, there was something else to fog it up. Sue got a couple chapters into the book of Acts, and found it to be so far over her head like a flying 747. She then looked at the clock and realized she needed to go to the kitchen and get supper started.

Sue's timing was perfect; she had just finished the potato salad when Dan walked in the door. After the fish were cleaned and grilled and their stomachs were full Sue said "Are you going to do some more fishing tomorrow?" "No, I think I will stay home and finish up some projects." What about you? Don't you have some shopping to do?" "Yes I do but the sale doesn't start until Monday. I still think you should go fishing while the weather is so nice."

On Sunday morning, Sue woke up early hoping Dan would change his mind, so she could get to church. She made homemade waffles with fresh strawberries and maple syrup, and fresh-squeezed orange juice. *That should get him fueled to go somewhere,* she thought. While he ate, Sue pumped him for any plans, but he wouldn't commit to anything and just kept asking what she was going to do. *He was gone yesterday, so I suppose he thinks it's my turn to do something; but I can't tell him what I want to do.* When it got to be ten o'clock, Sue just gave up.

\*　　\*　　\*

After lunch, Dan told Sue he was going into the den to read his Packers Preview paper that had just come in the mail. George followed him, and Dan was hoping George wasn't going to be a troublemaker. Dan hadn't even finished one article before George dropped the Bible on his lap. "Wait a minute, George. I want to finish reading about the Packers, and then I will read the Bible to you. Thank you for your obedience." Dan realized he was explaining his actions to a dog. *Maybe I can reason with God,* he

31

thought. He looked up and said, "Do you know how exciting it is to get all the latest info about the Packers? Maybe not. I think you and George are on the Bible-reading side. Okay, I am outnumbered; I will finish the paper later. But I want to find something equally exciting in the Bible." Dan then asked God, "Where should I read?" but he got no answer. Then he looked down and saw that the Bible was already opened to The Acts of the Apostles. "If you don't mind, God, I am going to call this The Touchdowns of the Apostles—just for now."

"We'll see what is a touchdown, a huddle, a foul, a first down, a field goal, and if anyone gets a penalty. Already we have a huddle—Captain Jesus told them to wait for the promise of the Father and they would receive power to win. Good pep talk with instructions and encouragement. With the crowd watching, Jesus went and made a touchdown, and then he kept going and disappeared into the clouds. It says he's going to come back the same way, so that will be another touchdown.

"At halftime, Jesus' team was on the sidelines and got some women to pray and supplicate with them. Peter said that Judas had left the game due to a penalty and needed to be replaced. They called Matthias. He put on his uniform and was ready to play.

"In the second half, it was very windy—so much so that Jesus' team got tongues of fire and were talking up a storm. There was no trash talk here; in fact, they were talking about God out on the field. That will do a number on an opposing team—and it did. They didn't know the language, but they understood each word as though it was English—but it wasn't. They were dumbfounded and called the ref and yelled 'Foul! The other team is drunk. They have to forfeit the game; we win.' Peter, the quarterback, got up right away and went over to the ref and said, "Our team is not drunk, as they accuse. They are just sore losers. We had visions of winning and just played them out."

Win they did, and afterward the losing team came up to Peter and asked, 'What should we do?' Then Peter said to them, 'Quit the other team and tell our captain you are sorry. Promise him you will play hard and do anything he asks, even if it looks or sounds foolish.' How is that, George? Do you think I could become a sportscaster?"

"Woof!"

"Okay, God, you got me away from my newspaper, and it was fun in the way you did it. Now I will read and be serious. But this looks more like a family than just a great team. They ate, prayed, believed, worshiped, and shared their wealth together. Sue and I haven't kept in touch with our families and even though I know that is wrong, it can't be changed. My dad was angry I didn't go to college, and then when he found out we couldn't give him a grandchild, he disowned me."

# Chapter Seven

Sue watched Dan pull out of the drive to go to work Monday morning. *Now I need to plan to get to church next Sunday. The dilemma continues, and the plot thickens. What plot? I can't plot against my own husband. Oh, but I am. I could tell him I am going to see a psychologist. As many people as Jesus healed, he could be just about any kind of doctor. I really want to go to church to find out about Dr. Jesus and whether he can help me, so it wouldn't be a lie. But would Dan believe I have a doctor's appointment on a Sunday morning? I doubt it, but I have to figure out something, because I am on a quest for answers and help. I have this life that is great on the outside, with a wonderful husband, a nice home, and my own car, and I can work when and if I want to. It sure looks like a fairytale life, but it isn't. I am miserable on the inside and have found nothing to change that. If this church can help even just a little bit, that will be great. Now that I think about, life has gotten better since I started reading the Bible.*

"Okay," Sue said with determination, "Today I'm going to go buy the whole Bible and maybe drive past that Love in Jesus church." The store wouldn't be open for another half hour, so she took George for a walk. No one was in sight, so she started talking to George. She said to him, "Why aren't there newspaper articles about God? I don't think I ever read one. Why would people want God out of government and schools if all he wants is to love every human being? Do these people think God is evil? From what I read, no matter how many people Jesus helped, there were always many people that hated him and tried to get rid of him. Is this why people don't read the Bible? George, if you could talk, I am sure you would have a lot to say."

Sue walked George back to the house and headed to the Christian Bookstore. She picked out a Bible and then began looking around. She spotted a book called *Can God Be Defined and Found?* She picked up a copy and went to the checkout counter.

Next, Sue headed to the church, and when she pulled into the parking lot, another car pulled in just ahead of her. When the woman in the car got out, Sue jumped out and asked her if she attended church there.

"Yes, I do. My name is Millie Murphy, and yes, my nickname is M&M."

Sue reached out her hand, with a smile on her face. "I'm Sue Frazier, and I am so glad to meet you. I am interested in attending a service here."

"That's great," Millie said. "You want to come this Sunday? In fact, why don't you come in and I will show you around?"

"No, thank you. I am interested in attending sometime soon, but I can't tell my husband, and I don't want to lie."

"I have an idea," said Millie, "but I would like to know why you chose this church, if you don't mind telling me."

"One day I was driving around checking out churches, and when I got here, I felt different—almost like I belonged here. And besides that, I loved the name."

Millie told Sue she had a plan that would work. "You tell your husband you are going to a meeting and you will be back in time to make him lunch."

"But what if he asks me what kind of meeting; then what do I say?"

"This is how it works: we will be praying that you will have favor with your husband, and he won't say anything and will just kiss you good-bye."

"But what if—"

"I believe everything will be just fine," said Millie. "God loves you, and we will see you Sunday."

Sue left and started on her way home, and then it hit her like a ton of bricks: *God loves me.* She started weeping and tried to stop, but the tears kept coming, so she pulled over and let them flow. For the first time ever, she really felt like God loved her. Once she was able to stop the tears, she continued home.

When Sue arrived, George greeted her with his usual tail-wagging, and she had to tell him what had happened. "George, I found out something so wonderful," she said. "God loves me." Saying it out loud made her start crying again. George gave her a couple of licks and then looked down toward the Bible/sewing room. "George, I have to start supper!" Sue danced her way to the kitchen, and George followed her, prancing. The big dog was trying to follow her dance steps, and it was a funny sight. Sue started laughing like she had never laughed before, and it sure felt good.

Sue went into the kitchen to make supper, which was going to be late. She was sure glad she had a nice, understanding husband. He was not the caveman type who would walk into the house demanding his supper. He would ask Sue if she needed help, and if she didn't give him a project right away, he would go to the den to read while he waited. It used to be football, basketball, or a fishing story (for example, one was about someone catching a big albino Muskie), but now it could be reading the Bible. *I wonder if we are reading the same thing and what he is learning. Has he discovered that God loves him?*

Sue finished preparing supper sooner than she thought she would. Dan arrived, and the two of them sat down to eat and had the usual conversations about their day—minus God. Dan said "you look different today, is it your hair, make-up or just the lighting?" "I would like to know if you mean different good or different bad." Dan quickly responded, "Definitely good." She thought that was so sweet, and she told him so. But she knew her appearance had to have changed because of the information she had received earlier that day. Her experience with the Bible was no longer just one of words; there was something else going on. Anyone can say he or she loves you, but when you realize that God really means it, that is entirely different.

# Chapter Eight

On Thursday afternoon, Dan told Stan he was planning to go to church on Sunday but just wasn't sure how. Stan told him to leave the details up to God and that it would all work out. That sounded almost too simple to him, but he had no other ideas. The only other thing Stan told him was to dress casual so he wouldn't be asked questions by his wife.

On Saturday, Dan and Sue went fishing. Dan didn't say much, because he didn't want to suddenly blurt out, "I am going to church tomorrow." He remembered doing that with a marriage proposal. He felt he just needed to wait for the right time; he would have to tell her something eventually.

They started out fishing with night crawlers and bobbers so they could drink their coffee. Dan's went down first, and he pulled out a nice bass. Then Sue caught one the same size; it could have been a twin, if there is such a thing in the fish world. While Dan was watching his bobber, he began thinking. *If that is how people are, just bouncing around in life, wandering, what is the purpose? Is that why I am reading the Bible? Yes. Are we just blobs that eventually die and that's the end, or is there a real meaning; and if there is, what is it? Is our life a test, and if it is, how good is good enough, and how bad is too bad?* He was snapped out of his thoughts by Sue yelling, "Get the net!" The fish on the end of her line was the biggest she had ever caught. They had enough for a meal and were done with their coffee, so they did some fly fishing, which they found fun because they could feel the fish as soon as they struck. When the fish showed no interest, they packed up to go home.

After a scrumptious fresh fish dinner, Dan was cleaning the grill, and Sunday was on his mind. Morning was just around the corner, and he still didn't know how he was going to get out of the house. He felt like a prisoner trying to plan an escape but not coming up with the details.

In bed that night, each of them noticed the other tossing and turning, but they said nothing. Neither one had a clue the other wanted to go to church. Dan had brought it up once, and there had been dead silence, so he never thought about Sue wanting to go. Sue thought that when Dan had brought it up, he was just doing it to try to get help for her but really didn't want to go himself.

# Chapter Nine

T he next morning, Sue was up early to make sure that breakfast was done, the dishes washed, and she could leave in plenty of time. Exactly at 9:30, she grabbed her purse, knocked on the door of the den without going inside, and said, "Dan, I am leaving now. I have a meeting to go to, and I will be back in time to make lunch. Dan came out and gave her a quick kiss and went back into the den. Sue got outside and shouted "Wow!" She drove all the way to church saying that one word over and over again. "Wow! Wow! Wow!"

\*   \*   \*

Meanwhile, as soon as the door closed, Dan watched out the window to see which way Sue was headed. Then he went and called Stan, who gave him the address and told him he would meet him at the door. He decided it would be best to go a different direction than Sue had gone in.

\*   \*   \*

Millie was waiting and Sue excitedly told her how easy it had been to get out of the house. Millie didn't act surprised, but she did say, "Wonderful. I am so glad you came."

When the service started, there was a band, and the songs they sang were happy songs about God. People clapped their hands and even had smiles on their faces. Sue thought to herself, *this is sure not how I pictured church.* The few times she had been in one, it had been solemn and sad. In this church they seemed to be happy. *These people must think God is good; otherwise, they wouldn't be smiling.*

After the singing, the pastor came to the podium in a baseball uniform, including a backward cap and a catcher's mitt, holding a Bible. "Okay, folks, this is it: the latest sports news! Jesus pitched a no-hitter; he struck out all of your sins. His home run covers all the bases of your life with his love. He will dust off home plate so you can clearly see his love and be at home in his arms. He will show you his fastball so you can strike out the Devil when he comes to bat you down." The pastor took off the cap and catcher's mitt and set them down. He then continued.

"A person ends up putting a dead bolt on their life, which keeps them captive. Jesus stands at the door and knocks. Just looking at him from the window of your life is not enough. First, prepare a place for Him by repenting of your sins. Then unlock the dead bolt, open the door, reach out, and welcome him. Jesus comes to a person with life-changing love and makes many blessings available."

Sue hung on every word the pastor spoke, and he was answering many of her questions. Jesus was looking more and more like the safe haven she had convinced herself didn't exist.

The pastor continued. "People may ask, 'How come all these horrible things are going on in this world if there is a loving God?' Yes, he could stop them if he made us all puppets and was controlling the strings of our life, but he isn't. After God created Adam and Eve he put them in the garden and told them to take dominion and subdue it. It was a place where there were no hardships, sicknesses or any other problems.

"When the serpent came to them, they had the freedom to listen to him or not. It was their garden; he was an intruder, and they should have kicked him out. God would not do it for them. All the Devil did was entice them to doubt God and offer them evil. They took the deal and people still fall for that same deal. When God confronted them, they both passed the buck and neither one repented. It is the same today; the further someone gets from God, the more they blame God. There are only two masters, and everyone is serving one or the other: Jesus, who is love; or Satan, who is hate.

"Now, to make sure you know, God does have wrath against evil, and what he said will come to pass. Everything God does is based in love and protection, and what the Devil does is based in hate and destruction. Even the flood happened to protect the human race from extinction. Mankind was so wicked that no one had even one kind word or one good thought—ever. It is hard to imagine one person, let alone every human being on the earth, was continuously evil. Noah was the only person in the whole world that would listen to God. He still looks for people who will listen and receive his love.

"If there is anyone here this morning that would like to meet Jesus, just raise your hand."

Sue put her hand up without even thinking about it.

I see that hand, and that one. Is there anyone else? Would those two people come up here and let me pray with them."

Sue got up and started down the aisle. As she was walking, someone took her hand. She turned to look and saw that it was Dan. They walked together, prayed together, and received Jesus together. They hugged each other, and the pastor shook their hands and sent them with a deacon to get some books and encouragement in their new walk with God. When they left the church, they realized they each had their own car and that they wouldn't be able to talk at length until they got home.

After a quick lunch, they sat down to share with each other all the developments that had happened to get them to church. They shared how they had both found out about the other one being into the Bible but hadn't said anything. They both had a good laugh, and then they hugged each other and started to cry, with laughter between the tears.

In the morning, Dan felt like he had a smile on his face to match Stan's, and he was excited about going to work. When he walked past the den, he stopped and grabbed his Bible. He said to it, "You may get me some sneers, name callings, and people not liking me, but I am going to be proud to carry you." When Dan got to the end of the hall, Sue was waiting at the door with a smile, a good-bye kiss, and his lunch. He got into his truck, and before he could turn the key, tears started to well up that were hard to fight. "God, I think I just witnessed my first miracle! In all the years I have been married, I have never seen what I just saw. My wife looked peaceful, happy, and full of life, and it was really real. I've watched a whole lot of phony, but this came from her heart. Now I ask that you heal her of her past."

"My Heavenly Father, I want you to know I am taking my Bible to work. I am reporting for duty by enlisting in your army, and being in your boot camp. My dad taught me how to take orders, and that's just what I will do. One other thing: I am not the serious kind, so can we keep having fun? Like your visits to my basement, which were funny and serious at the same time? You really had me going. It would have made a great newspaper headline: "Dan Frazier Gets Bargain Basement Visit from God" or "Fisherman's Dream: God's Love Bait." How about your own newspaper column called Answers from the Top? The first one could be "Jesus Soul Wash—Removes Sins."

At work, Dan found Stan right away, who shook his hand and welcomed him into God's family. Dan said he had a question. "Stan, how come you never said anything to me?"

"Oh, but I did; I said 'Jesus.' Each person is different, and with you that was all I needed to say; God was going to do the rest. Christianity is not something someone can be taught; it's about pointing to God and his word so the person looks to and seeks Jesus."

\*     \*     \*

The phone rang just as Sue finished lunch, and it was Millie, wanting to check on her and see if she had any questions. Sue said, "I am having the best day ever, but God's actions in the Bible still seem to be mixed."

"I know exactly what you mean," said Millie. "Then I found out everything has to line up with the words of Jesus. Just go to John 10:10 and it will keep you on the right track."

Sue said, "Millie, you helped me a lot today. I see where Satan gets away with stuff and then blames God so a person is stuck with no one to turn to. That is how I lived." After Sue hung up, she thought, *maybe someday soon I will be strong enough to share my secret with Dan.*

# Chapter Ten

In the days and weeks ahead, Dan and Sue rarely missed their "God experience" together each evening, and in church they were learning that God was really worthy of their worship and praise. When they first joined Love in Jesus Fellowship, they mostly watched people and just sang the songs as they were learning the words. One Sunday morning, Pastor John explained worship: "it is when someone claims to be in love with you, and you don't just want kind words and occasional attention, but you really want their heart. When you have someone's heart, there is a dedication, a commitment, a desire to spend time with you and give to you, more than to anything or anyone else. Church is not about coming and singing a few songs, listening to a sermon, paying tithes, and going home. It is like a young romantic couple with a special meeting place. Each plans around, looks forward to, and can hardly wait to see the other person, who has become the center of their life. That is when worship and everything about God becomes exciting. It is fun to be with someone you love and who loves you back." Sue and Dan were so hungry to learn about God's love, they had become like two baby birds that were hungry again as soon as they were fed. The more they learned about and experienced God's love, the more they wanted.

That great love is not to be left at church; it is to be lived and operated in. It produced some changes at work for Dan and his friend Stan. At first they didn't realize what was going on, but eventually it dawned on both of them. Dan would be sitting, reading his Bible across from Stan, and he would tell him to turn to a particular verse. "Isn't that exciting? I didn't know that; did you know that?" After a few times, they noticed some nearby ears straining to find out just what could be so exciting in the Bible. All human beings are naturally curious.

One day after work, Dan got into his truck and Stan came over to discuss the guys that were listening and pretending not to. "Let's have some fun with this. How about when one of us finds something neat, we will start out speaking a little loud like we have been doing, but then let's get a little quieter when we come to the main part. God's punch line, so to speak. God has called us to be as wise as serpents and as harmless as doves. So let's see if we can't bend some ears far enough that they will fall right into God's arms."

After supper that evening, Sue came into the den and told Dan she wanted to talk to him. Dan put his newspaper down and looked at her. "You know I never told anyone about my past," she said. "I will try to tell you, but I don't know if I can."

"When I was little it seemed like I had a wonderful childhood. My parents were in love, and they loved me. They took me on picnics, fishing, flying kites, and they taught me a lot of things, like knitting, cooking, gardening, and even how to clean a fish. I was an only child, so I was the center of their lives." Then there was a long pause, and Sue started shaking. As she spoke, her voice cracked. She continued in a whisper. "Everything crashed when I was twelve and was raped by a relative. Weeks later, I found out I was pregnant. Because of who did it I couldn't tell anyone, so I felt I had to have an abortion. Now, because of that, I can never have children. There is so much more, but I can't finish the story now. It is just too horrible." Dan held his wife for a long time before her tears stopped.

*How could there possibly be more?* Dan thought. He already wanted to find this guy and kill him, but being a Christian, he knew that wasn't the answer. He said to God, "Couldn't I just work this guy over and make him feel some pain? God, I need to do something: what can I do?"

Sue ended up feeling worse in a way, because she now knew that at some point she would have to tell Dan the rest, and she didn't know what he might do. She already sensed hostility in Dan and knew he could explode. *What if he did something bad to them? Then I would have to live with that too.* They went to bed without either one saying anything, but each knew the other wasn't sleeping.

The next morning, Dan selfishly wished it was a work day—not because he didn't want to be with Sue, but he just didn't know what he could say or do to help her. After breakfast, Sue took her Bible and sat outside by the garden. She found solace in just looking around and seeing the beauty around her. Then she let her mind wander to what had happened the night before, and then the past did another TV-style rerun. She couldn't find a way to turn it off, so a new supply of tears came streaming down her face.

She had opened a can of worms and now knew why she had wanted to keep everything buried. She felt suppressed pain was easier to deal with than exposed pain.

Just then the phone rang. Sue answered and found it was Tom's wife, Pam, wanting to know if there was anything they could bring when they came over that evening. Sue composed herself and said, "Dan has everything set, including the chicken that's marinating. What you can do is bring some games for after we eat."

Pam told Sue they had recently bought a new Bible game in which players tried to get from Genesis to Revelations by answering two questions from each book. "They are multiple choices, so that makes it easier. There is a one-minute timer. If you don't answer correctly, it goes to the next person, and when it gets back around, you have to stay in the same book until you get two questions right. I think it was designed to help us new Christians get started, and maybe to challenge older ones."

Sue said, "It sounds like fun." She got off the phone feeling better and looking forward to the evening.

\*    \*    \*

Dan arrived home from last minute shopping, just in time to get the chicken on the grill. He gave Sue a big hug and asked her how she was doing. She told him she was doing better and was glad they were having company.

The neighbors arrived right on time. During the meal, Sue could tell that they sensed something was wrong, but she hoped the Bible game would help with that. When they set up the game, there were new rules added. Everyone would get two minutes instead of one, and they could use their Bibles and a concordance. This helped each of them advance through the Bible, and they all learned a lot. When their neighbors went home, Sue went over and hugged her husband and told him what a wonderfully fun evening it had been. Lying in bed Dan watched his wife sleeping peacefully, but his mind would not stop questioning. "What else happened that she can't tell me? How could there possibly be more? Do I even want to know?

\*    \*    \*

In the following weeks, Sue and Dan both noticed even more changes in themselves and in each other. Dan noticed Sue was becoming more and more relaxed with her walk with the Lord.

After many Bible studies and lots of praying, Sue decided to tell Dan everything. She called him up from the basement and told him she felt she was strong enough in the Lord to tell him, and he told her he was ready to listen and help her in any way he could. They sat in the den, and Sue looked at Dan and started. "When I told you about the rape and the abortion, there was a lot more to the story, and I am not sure I have everything—or much of anything—straight. But this is my understanding from what I saw and heard which were only bits and pieces."

"As I told you, my life was going along very nicely until one night. My dad didn't come home for supper and didn't call. My mom was worried, but she tried to hide it from me. I thought maybe something had happened to him, and my mom got tired of my questions and sent me to bed. While I lay in bed, I heard the back door close but didn't hear any voices, so I figured it was my mom going to look for my dad. I eventually fell asleep.

"The next thing I knew, my dad was on top of me, tearing off my clothes. I tried to scream, and nothing came out. All I remember is the horrible pain and the smell of alcohol. Afterward, he left and walked out the door. I heard his car drive away. I tried to convince myself it was not my dad. It just couldn't have been my father; he would never hurt me, and he never drank. But I knew it was him. I got up and took a bath and changed. I looked through the house and saw no sign of my mom. So I wrapped up the bloody clothes, put them in a bag, and took them out to the garbage. Then I went and turned on the TV and just stared at it, waiting for my mom to come home.

"When she finally did come home, she asked if Dad had called, and I said no. She told me she didn't think he was ever coming back. I asked why, and she said she couldn't talk about it now. I could tell she had been crying. I went and put my arms around her, but I really needed her arms around me. During the next weeks, a neighbor—Bill Grayson, whose wife had divorced him about a year before—seemed to be hanging around a lot. When he and his wife were together, they spent a lot of time with my parents. At some point, even as a young child, I noticed Bill looking at my mother in a way that gave me an uneasy feeling. Being a little kid, I just forgot about it. When I inquired as to why Bill was coming over so often, my mom just shrugged it off and said he was just being a friend at a very difficult time. She never heard from my dad and had no clue where he was. For weeks after this happened, I would still hear my mom say, 'What happened? What did I do?' This was all very confusing to me. It led me to believe my parents hadn't even fought, yet everything went wrong.

"With all this going on, I didn't notice I missed my period, but I noticed my clothes started to get a little tight. I tried to dismiss it, but I knew I was pregnant. I had to do something before my mom noticed. There was no way I could tell her anything. A friend of mine who had recently had an abortion was able to help me get one without having to get my mother involved. It was a horrible ordeal and didn't seem to go very well, but I didn't ask any questions. The plan was to stay at my friend's for the weekend. Her folks were out of town, and I sat around and cried a lot.

"Sunday night I had to go back home and act like everything was normal. But inside, the pain was unbearable. It is one thing to be hurt by someone that is not close to you, but my dad was my idol. How would I ever again be able to trust anyone? My mom seemed to be doing pretty good and was spending more and more time with our neighbor Bill. Watching what was going on with my mom worked as a distraction for me. To my knowledge she never called the police to file a missing persons report or even called around to try to locate my father. As much as she loved my dad, she just stopped even talking about him—like he never existed. Bill always came around to comfort her, and then after a time, he claimed he loved her and they got married. This never set right with me.

"I was really baffled, because my parents had really been in love. They had their little spats, but right from the beginning of their marriage they had an agreement—in fact, I was told this was even in their marriage vows—that any disagreement would have to be solved before they went to bed that night and not brought up again.

"Nothing was adding up, and I had this detective instinct, so I started listening and watching to try to get a clue as to what really happened. Bill tried to act like a father to me, and at first I was very standoffish. I no longer wanted any kind of dad. But once I started my investigation, I figured I needed to be nice to him so maybe he would let his guard down enough that I would find something out.

"It took a few months, and I still never got any concrete evidence, but I felt I had enough pieces of the puzzle that what I filled in wasn't too far off. My parents had looked at Bill and Kate as trusted friends for many years. Bill's hidden—or should I say not-so-hidden—feelings for my mom may have been a factor in his divorce. I don't know. But it would stand to reason that once Pam left Bill, he had more time to be jealous of the great marriage my folks had, and he set out to ruin it. Somewhere along the way, he was no longer interested in a friendship with my dad and just wanted his wife. Since he had been a trusted friend, he could tell my dad anything and my dad would believe him.

"The only thing that could break up my parents' marriage was if one cheated on the other. That is what Bill must have used. He told my dad my mom was cheating on him and told my mom my dad was cheating on her. All he did was patiently wait for the right moment so they would be hurt at the exact same time and nothing would ever get straightened out.

"Believing that information, my dad must have snapped. When people have a rocky marriage, they can usually see something like this coming. But my dad was blindsided and couldn't deal with it. He was not a drinker, but he went out and got drunk enough to not know what he was doing. I am guessing he came to humiliate my mother for what she had done by raping her and then walking out.

"The only way my mom wouldn't have been frantic and called the police is if she had stopped at Bill's to see if he had seen her husband and she was told a similar story. Maybe he told her he had seen my dad with another woman and they had both had suitcases in hand.

"If this is even close to right, it looks like Bill got away with it. My hands are tied. First of all, I don't have any proof. Plus, on the rare occasion I talk to my mom, she and Bill seem to be at least somewhat happy. If I say anything, everything in her world will explode and she will blame me for her losing the little bit of happiness she has. If I look for my dad to try to get the truth and I find out I am even close to right, I have no clue as to what he might do to Bill. Besides, I don't know if I could face him, because I really don't know what happened for sure. Part of me thinks that when he sobered up he figured out what he did and that's why he never came back. He just couldn't face me. Otherwise, why wouldn't he have fought for full custody or at least visitation rights?"

Sue hadn't been facing Dan while she was speaking. She turned to him and saw the pain in his face and could tell he had been crying. "Maybe I shouldn't have told you any of this and made you have to carry it around. That's not fair. What do we do with all this now that we are Christians?"

Dan put his arms around Sue. He didn't answer right away because his head was still spinning with all that he had heard. After thinking about it for what seemed like a long time, he said to Sue, "Let's not say or do anything right now? We will pray together and ask for God's wisdom, guidance, and direction." By the time they finished praying and reading the Bible, they were both doing better and glad it was bed time.

Sue couldn't fall asleep and was not sure she had done the right thing. It sure didn't make her feel any better at all. But she was more convinced that what she had told Dan was at least close to the truth. Through the years, thoughts had developed in her mind that made it worse, such as her dad hating her. She thought she must have done something so bad that he didn't want anything to do with her and that the attack was his last punishment before leaving for good. Even after she started some investigating and was leaning toward the account she gave Dan, other stories, more gruesome, would play in her mind. She was glad she hadn't told him any of them. Sue finally drifted off to sleep when she made her mind think about how much God loves her.

Monday morning brought a new work week, and Dan was glad. His tough maleness was trying to figure out how to handle the news of what his wife had gone through. Seeing Stan and doing their day's planning sure helped. They referred to themselves as God's Spider Duo. The plan was to weave the word of God in front of their fellow workers and pray they would wisely receive Jesus. It seemed like the quieter they talked, the more some of the guys strained to hear.

On his way home from work, Dan's thoughts turned to his wife. For all those years, he didn't know what to say because he didn't know what was wrong. Now that he knew, he still didn't know what to say. He just walked in the house, ate supper, and helped Sue clean up and get ready for an evening of games with their neighbors.

After one game of cribbage, they all wanted to play the Bible game, using the New Testament. Dan and Sue were surprised at how many verses they remembered. When they got to the book of Ephesians, one of the questions was, "Which of the Ten Commandments has a promise attached to it?" They guessed the first because that was the most important one. It was quite a shock to learn they were wrong. They were even more surprised to find out it was the fourth: the commandment to love and honor your mother and father. Those commandments were given a long time ago, and realistically most people can't keep them all and have very good reasons they can't. People Dan and Sue had talked to had lots of good reasons not to obey this one. Many people visit parents to pay their dues without really wanting to. Dan and Sue didn't even do that, with all the circumstances involved with their parents. But this sure made them both squirm a little.

Because it was such a fast-paced game, that subject was quickly buried, and many new ones appeared. All four players did fairly well until the book of Revelations; no one found an answer on the first try. It wasn't until the fourth or fifth try that they began to get correct answers. The evening ended with everyone agreeing they had a lot to learn.

# Chapter Eleven

One evening sitting outside Sue said to Dan, "It looks like fall is earlier than usual. Look at the leaves. They speak there is a creator. There are so many shapes, colors and shades which we get to enjoy and then watch them all die and fall off. Then in spring, new ones appear." Dan added, "Just like leaves, people come is all shapes, colors, and sizes. Even though they may look beautiful on the outside, they are dying on the inside." "I see what you mean, when a person is born again by receiving Jesus, then the leaves (old life) die and new leaves (new life) begin." "Yes we are brand new leaves."

Dan laughed and said, "Fun is more fun with God. Let's make a big pile of leaves and jumped in it and roll around." "Great idea, do you think making leaf angels would work like snow angels do?" After playing for a while Sue said, "I'm going in the house to make hot apple cider." Dan said, "Good, I am getting thirsty, I will form two lounge chairs out of leaves". He and Sue sat on their leaf chairs, enjoyed their drinks, and looked around their yard to see what changes or additions they would make the following spring.

Sunday morning was church, and Dan and Sue acted like two little kids going to a birthday party as they drove to attend the service. "What a special time of visiting with someone we know and love and who loves us very much," said Dan. "People that don't know Jesus yet may have the same thoughts we had. Who wants to visit a stranger, especially one that has a reputation for bringing wrath and punishment? It's like a child not wanting to face a parent when they have been naughty." They arrived at church not knowing that Pastor John's sermon was going to be a setup for freedom they never thought possible. He started out as usual by reassuring the congregation of God's great love. "Changes don't come in our live through the law, but through God's love. We can't earn anything. Jesus did it all and his grace is always enough. We just recognize and respond to his love. Do you want bondage in self-justification or freedom in God's love?"

"That was the introduction. Today's sermon is titled "All about Leeches . . . ." I think I have your attention. The question is do you have them? And do you want to keep them, or are you willing to do whatever it takes to get rid of your leeches?"

"I wanted to make this graphic so you would not only hear, but also see, what could be happening to you. Leeches are bloodsucking worms that attach themselves and consume three times their weight. Did something happen in your past that sucked life out of you and you are still carrying that weight?"

"Most people, when they receive Jesus into their life, come with lots of baggage. They will adamantly tell you all about their hurt and anger and say that it is justified. Could those facts be your leeches? God disposes facts through the shed blood of Jesus, so he is free to love us. To continue to be graphic, it's like he flushes our sins down the toilet, never to be seen or mentioned again . . . . Today I am here to tell you there is a higher law than the facts. The fact: Mary was a virgin and could not be pregnant—but she was. All this is leading up to this question: how many of you can truthfully say you fully love and honor your mother and father and have no bad thoughts or facts against them?"

There were only a few hands raised in that wonderful Christian church.

"How many would like to obey God and enjoy his promises?"

Every hand went up. "Good! There are going to be three classes on God's commandment with promise. They will start this Tuesday at 7:00 p.m. What good is the word of God if it isn't powerful enough to set you free?"

"Sometimes obeying God is something that we either don't want to do or figure there is no way to do. So people just erase those passages from their mind. If we eliminated everything that people chose not to believe, felt wasn't for today or didn't apply to them, or found simply impossible to do, we would have about ten pages left of the Bible, and that would be mostly the 'begats.' Your homework is to practice saying—in your mind and out loud—"I love and honor my father and mother." You may feel like you are lying, but feelings don't count when it comes to Gods freedom."

On the way home, Dan and Sue had many questions: How do you block out, erase, ignore, or get rid of the facts of what really happened? How do you love someone that has hurt you beyond repair? Will anyone come to the meeting Tuesday evening? Dan said he was going to the meeting, and Sue decided to join him even if they were the only ones there.

Over lunch they decided they needed a three-day weekend to try not to think about what God was requiring of them. Sue said, "Maybe we could look for my dad."

"And maybe we could do something special for my parents," said Dan. "Will you listen to us? Only one class and we are thinking about the impossible."

Dan arrived at work early on Monday morning hoping to talk to Stan, but he couldn't find him. At lunch he met Stan at what some of the guys called "the Bible table." There were four sets of ears listening. Stan told him he had been out of town for the weekend, and that was why he hadn't been in church Sunday. As Dan filled Stan in on what he had missed, three guys left, leaving one remaining. His name was Frank, and he asked us to write down the address of the church and service time. On Tuesday, Sue was ready and had supper on the table when Dan walked in. He inquired if she was in a hurry to get to church, and she answered, "Yes, it is either going to be really packed or really empty." They were learning that when it comes to what God commands, he provides the grace for us to do it.

Church didn't start until 7:00, but they arrived at 6:15 to find it half full already. At ten to seven, Dan was setting up extra chairs in any available space, including the foyer.

Service started with glorious praise and worship. Afterward, Pastor John greeted everyone and reminded them how much God loves us. All you have to do is accept what God has already done and then he will make a way for you to enjoy his promises. No one can earn salvation but when a person accepts Jesus they enjoy what he has done. God doesn't command us to do anything that he doesn't provide the way to get it done. We are going to look very closely at 'Honor thy Father and thy Mother, as the Lord thy God hath commanded thee; that thy days may be prolonged, and that it may go well with thee, in the land which the Lord thy God giveth thee.' There are always blessings in obeying God, so why was he so specific, and why did he attach such big promises to this one? "I hope to answer this question in a way that you will understand, and I hope you will be willing to throw out all facts and excuses, obey God, and receive his blessings. I am sure that if I interviewed a hundred people as to why they didn't love and honor their mother and father, I would get a big variety of answers, but each one would come down to 'They don't deserve it. Some may say we are no longer under the law. That is true. But if you are still suffering under the law then it needs to be dealt with.'

"When we invite Jesus into our life, in a split second we go from hell bound to heaven bound. In that same split second, God takes all of our sins and throws them into the sea of forgetfulness and remembers them no more. If he remembers them no more, they are erased from his mind. If we try to bring them up, God will tell us he doesn't know what we are talking about. He has absolutely no record of them. Compare that to how many times you have heard or even said, "I will forgive but never forget. We would all be in big trouble if God would be thinking about and reminding us of our sins forever. Remember, if you haven't forgotten, then you really haven't forgiven. If he can forgive *and* forget, we can too.

"I remember getting a speeding ticket once, and it was while I was passing a small truck. I would guess most people don't look at their speedometer while trying to proceed safely and quickly around another vehicle. Instead of just sending in payment, I traveled sixty miles to try to get my fine reduced. I sat through every case and was never called. I was the only one left, and I handed them my paperwork, which proved I was speeding. They informed me that they had no record, so therefore I was free to go and it would never be brought up again. As far as the court was concerned, I never did anything wrong—even though I had proof that I did.

"Remember, this is not Gods suggestion it is how he demands you see them. He also says we are to owe no man anything, but to love them. He wants us to love everyone, but there are only two people that qualify to get the great promises for each of us doing so. This indicates that God puts a high priority on loving and honoring your father and mother. Why is this so very important for everyone to do?"

"I am going to end this here and continue in two weeks with the answer. I don't want this to be just another sermon you file somewhere in your subconscious and not deal with. That is why this is ongoing—so it is brought to the surface and dealt with in one of two ways: with obedience and blessings, or with continued disobedience and pain. Those of you that think you have no choice but the latter will find out there is always a choice to do something God's way. In our lives, we are continually walking through doors, and we pick them. Satan leaves his doors wide open, with all kinds of temptations. God's doors are narrow, but that is only because you can't walk through them without him. He meets you at the door, ready to take your hand and teach you and guide you in his way, which is the right way.

"Tonight has been the main course, and the next meeting will be dessert. It will taste good to obey God. Continue with loving thoughts and words about your parents. Your additional homework is to take a pencil and draw a pile of trash and then draw two people. If you are not much of an artist draw stick people. Now erase the trash, which represents your parent's sins. With those gone there is absolutely no reason not to love and honor your Mother and Father.

Dan and Sue stayed about an hour to pray and then left to go home. Even though they believed everything their pastor said, their minds still played their pasts in 3-D, widescreen, with the volume up. Every evening, they did their homework and went over their notes and Bible verses from Tuesday. Dan's mind told him he could do this, but for Sue the past had such strong roots that even yanking and hollering and erasing them didn't seem to make them budge. What kept them both determined was the knowledge that God would not tell them to do something that was impossible to do. One neighbor who had been at the services came over and shared what he had learned. "What many children go through is so horrible. It is generally, in actual time, a small part of their life, but the horror can be carried around for a lifetime of sixty, seventy, eighty years or more. The carrying actually ends up hurting them worse than the thing that happened, because it takes away their freedom to ever really enjoy life."

# Chapter Twelve

The three-day weekend vacation arrived. Everything was done ahead of time except the decision of where to go. Dan blindfolded Sue and spun her around; they would travel in whatever direction she stopped. She ended up facing west. They had loaded up the car with fishing tackle, hiking clothes, and walking sticks. The cooler was full of water, sandwiches, and apples. Before pulling out of the driveway, they asked the Lord to take them on a fun adventure.

After traveling across town and down some county roads, they spotted an old gravel road and decided to see where it led. First they found enjoyment in seeing some cows grazing; then they had to stop the car for some chickens to cross the road. They were awed by a farmhouse with an old gray barn. "There is something about barns that is so attractive," said Sue. "It can be the finely maintained red ones with a horse-head weather vane on top or an old, abandoned gray barn that hasn't been used in many years. Both have equal beauty."

After looking around for a while Dan added. "Another fun thing to see is the old, rusty farm equipment that looks like it was just parked at its last place of usefulness and left there. It is calling to city folks to guess what it is, how it was used, and how old it is. Usually people will contemplate for a moment or two, and then it is on to the next sight, around the next bend. Generally, farm houses were not much to look at, which could be because they were mostly places to eat and sleep. Where farmers really lived was out caring for their animals and land. In the spring, they would plant these perfect rows of corn, wheat, or whatever. When things started to grow it looked like the farmer had taken a measuring stick and planted each row in perfect alignment to the next. Nowadays it is machinery that does that, but back then it was just part of being a good farmer. At harvest time they would have to walk those rows to pick their crops."

When they got back on pavement, their goal was to find another gravel road and a place to eat their lunch. After traveling down another county road, they almost missed what they were looking for because there was so much brush. If it had been summer, all the thick greenery would have kept it well hidden. It looked like it might be intended only for local people. But there was no sign that said "Private," so they assumed it was a public road. They turned and started down it, and as they came around the first curve, there in its entire splendor was a flock of turkeys. They couldn't tell if the turkeys were welcoming them or making a roadblock, but as the car got closer, they took off.

A little farther down the road was a large herd of cows. Sue suggested having a moo-moo contest. Dan had to ask, "What in the world is a moo-moo contest?"

"I know this is going to sound strange, but we wanted to have fun, and I think it would be interesting to see who could make a cow moo first. Besides, there is no one around."

Dan said, "Okay, as long as you won't tell anyone. I don't want to get flooded with mooing requests." They got out of the car, went over by the fence, and set up the rules. Sue went first. She figured that with around fifty cows, it should be pretty easy. Her first moo was long but not very loud and not even one cow looked in her direction. Dan was very confident and felt he would give an authoritative and strong moo, which he did. He managed to get a couple of heads to turn, and he got one to make a cow pie, but that was it. After about twenty minutes of all kinds of mooing and other sounds, they started to laugh and gave up. Sue said, "What do us city folks know? Maybe cows only moo at certain times of the day." They got back in the car and just when they were about to pull away, one cow came over by the fence and mooed.

They continued down the road, and they noticed what looked like a path. They stopped to check it out, and on the side was a little sign that read "Goose Neck Trail." It was around noon, so they decided to take their lunch and walking sticks and let the fun begin. Like good scouts, they had a compass along, and they marked their trail. After about an hour of walking, they found a big fallen tree to sit on while eating lunch. The only animals they had seen were a couple of squirrels and some chipmunks.

They had just started to eat the sandwiches when Dan saw something dark out of the corner of his eye, and he slowly turned to see a black bear with her cub. The bears were right on the trail Dan and Sue had just come from, so they had not only Dan and Sue's scent but also the smell of the delicious sandwiches. "Sue," Dan said nervously, "There are bears back there. Don't even look. Just slowly put your food down and walk slowly in the opposite direction of where they are. Don't run, and don't panic. Hopefully they will be interested in our food and leave us alone." They watched them, and Dan and Sue kept their eyes on the bears as they cautiously backed away. When Dan and Sue were far enough away but still in sight, the bears walked over to the food, and began enjoying it.

Dan and Sue didn't realize that in their backward flight, they had ended up at someone's house. Just as they were discussing their options, a voice from behind them asked, "Can I help you?"

A startled Dan and Sue spun around to see a middle-aged man standing on a porch. They explained about the sign, eating lunch, and the bears. He introduced himself. "I'm Jake, and you folks come on in for a spell until those bears leave." They gladly took him up on his offer. He informed them the bears had been eating his berries all summer and shouldn't attack out of hunger, but only out of defense of a cub or themselves. They told him they were city folks and would just as soon not be that close. Dan asked about the Goose Neck Trail sign and if they were on private land. Jake said, "Yes and no. If you would have walked just a little farther, you would have found Lake Alto. That is a public lake, but most of the land around it is private."

"Before I moved here, some agreement was made with the government that a trail could be here, but not a road. So there is a small amount of public access. With only a trail, folks would have to walk in or use a four-wheeler. That means not too many people know about it, so there is still privacy. I don't advertise, but I have a couple of rowboats I occasionally rent out." Sue asked if he minded if she asked some questions, and Jake said, "Go ahead, and I will answer them if I can." She was curious as to how he went shopping and other places. He told her he had a four-wheeler he rode to his truck. Dan said they didn't see any truck and that he hoped it wasn't stolen. Jake laughed. "It is there. I just let nature make me a little garage, right by the road. I usually go into town once or twice a month, to shop and get my mail."

"How long have you lived here?" Dan asked.

"Around fifteen years ago this place went up for sale, and it was everything I needed, so here I am."

"Do you do any fishing on Lake Alto, and do you know how it got its name?"

"Story goes that the man who first settled here, claimed this lake as his, and decided to name it. He had a son who loved playing the saxophone. He preferred that his son help him in farming and taking care of the animals, but his wife talked him into letting their son develop a little culture. He agreed, as long as it wasn't more than a half hour a day. When he got fairly good, he told his dad he was going to play for the fish. Then they would multiply and grow faster so they could have more fish dinners.

"There didn't seem to be many fish in the lake, so his dad rarely bothered to fish, but he humored his son and said, 'If that works, I will let you play your sax for an hour a day.' The boy had a plan and went out faithfully every day and played for the fish. He even built a little shanty so he could still play in the rain or snow. After about a year of this, he had a little free time on his birthday and decided to do some fishing. About an hour later, he proudly took his catch to show his father. The boy had a nice stringer of walleye and bass. The dad had never thought much of his son's alto sax, but now he was changing his mind. The following afternoon, he took his son down to the lake and uncovered a sign he had made that read 'Lake Alto.' His son liked that but was far more excited that he'd get to play another half hour each day. The fishing got so good that the boy's father was able to sell some of the land around the lake for a huge profit. The son went on to play in some touring bands and eventually taught music."

Jake apologized for being so long-winded, but Dan and Sue agreed they loved the story. Dan asked how the fishing was now, and if they could do some. Jake answered, "Rumor has it that when the boy left home, the really good fishing left too. Now it has become like most lakes; on a really good day, you can still catch a nice stringer of fish. To answer your other question, yes, you can fish, and you can even use one of my boats. There is also plenty of room to camp if you want to do that too." Dan said that sounded great, but he told Jake they hadn't brought their tent and that he wasn't sure if he'd want to camp with bears around. Jake offered them his tent and said he would leave his hound outside with them.

Dan and Sue had wanted an adventure, and this sure qualified, so they agreed. Jake let them use his four-wheeler to go back and get their stuff. They also drove to town to get some food. They picked out three nice steaks, assorted veggies to grill, and a few other things, including some marshmallows—just in case.

They arrived back at the house to find Jake had the tent all set up and there was just enough daylight left to make the meal, eat it, and clean up the mess. Jake said, "I learned early on not to leave any food out, or I could wake up to a zoo outside my back door. Besides, you don't want to make wild animals too friendly. That's another story." Dan and Sue chimed in to say that they loved his stories and wanted to hear more. He said, "If you folks would like, I can build a nice, big bonfire and we can sit around and tell stories. The only thing I don't have is marshmallows." Sue lifted up the bag that they had bought.

While the guys tended to the fire, Sue set up everything in the tent. Jake supplied them with sleeping bags, a small heater, and flashlights.

After they had all sat down by the warm fire, they asked Jake about the story he had made reference to at suppertime. Jake told them that it had come to mind earlier and was about an animal that didn't live around there. "It took place in Florida while I was staying with some friends, and it is their story. They lived on five acres in a little town named Upside Down Hill, which is another story. Anyway, they had three small children and two ponds with gators in them. Of course, the top priority was to protect their children. As long as the gators were afraid, they could stay. If they got even the least bit brave, they had to be captured and removed from the premises. Living here in the middle of nowhere; my policy has always been 'do not feed the animals,' because one day they could become friendly enough to mistake me for their lunch."

Sue said to Jake, "You really know how to tell interesting stories. I bet your family loves that. Do they live close by?" At that moment, a serious expression crossed Jake's face, and his head hung down. Sue apologized right away, saying, "I am sorry; I didn't mean to get personal."

"I live here because my family doesn't want me. It's all right; I am doing okay." But his tears told Sue he wasn't doing okay. Jake told them that his life was a pretty sad story and that he didn't want to bore them with it. Dan and Sue said that they were on vacation and had plenty of time to listen. They thought maybe they could help because they personally knew the Great Helper.

Jake began his story. "I guess my life was never very good, but it took a major nose dive when I was ten and my parents split up. Part of divorce for kids is that they generally watch their parents fight over them, and the children become confused as to what is going to happen and whose side they should be on. In my case, neither one of my parents wanted me. I felt like I was thrown back and forth like a stinky piece of garbage. It leaves a child feeling worthless when your own parents don't want you and don't even try to hide that fact from you." Jake got up and walked out of the room, leaving Dan and Sue in tears. After a few minutes, he returned, apologized, and continued.

"My father's parents owned a farm, and they came and looked me over. They decided I was getting big and could do enough work to earn my keep, so they took me in. Actually, the next eight years weren't too bad. Living on the farm was nice, even though the work was hard. School gave me a break, when they would let me go, and I really enjoyed learning. My grandparents didn't show me any affection, but they took care of me. I tried not to get into any trouble because they were also very strict. Sometimes while I was busy repairing a fence or cleaning out the barn, I would daydream about what I wanted to do when I got old enough to leave. The animals on the farm became my best friends, so I thought of becoming a veterinarian.

"I was a loner all through high school. My life was tied to a never-ending list of chores waiting for me. During lunch breaks, I occasionally sat next to this girl named Emily. There was an attraction to her, mostly because I somehow sensed that her life wasn't good either. What happened was that in the little time we spent together, not much was said, because neither of us wanted to bore the other with their life.

"The week after I graduated from high school, my grandparents were killed in a terrible car accident. It devastated me. Even though we weren't close, they were all the family I'd had for the last eight years. At the funeral, I looked for my parents, but neither one showed up. I did get to meet some aunts, uncles, and cousins that I didn't even know I had. A few days later, when I was contemplating what to do, I got a call from my grandparents' lawyer. He informed me that I had inherited the farm and all of its contents. The will said that seeing as I had worked all those years, I was the best one to take care of it. I wish they would have left it to me because they loved me, but that wasn't in there." Jake got a little choked up and paused. Then he said, "Hey! It's getting late, and you must be bored with all of this." Sue said, "No, please continue, I am wide awake," and Dan agreed. So Jake contained himself and went on.

"This was more responsibility than I wanted or knew how to handle. I turned to the only person I could think of, and that was Emily. She responded to me with kindness, and because of that kindness I asked her to marry me, and she said yes. I didn't see it at the time, but it was a marriage of desperation for both of us. She never said much, but I surmised her upbringing had been even worse than mine. Neither one of us knew anything about love, so we had none to give.

"After eight years of marriage and four children, we were both done. We couldn't give each other or our children something we didn't have. Not wanting them to experience the same thing I had, where neither parent wanted them, I just walked out. Now I know it was wrong, but at the time, I was so worthless inside that I felt I was sparing them from living with a broken shell of a man. I took off and went back to Florida to live.

"With all the maintenance I had learned on the farm, I had no problem getting a job. I left Emily the farm and sent cards, letters, and money for her and the kids but never heard anything back. I worked long hours and had minimal expenses, so I was able to save some money. Eventually I came back here and bought this place. I hoped that someday my kids would come and see me, but that hasn't happened. It looks like I will end my life the same way I lived it—alone."

Now the tears were streaming down Sue's face. Even Dan had some tears welling up, but he was able to hold them back. Jake noticed and apologized, and he said he was going to go to bed. Sue said, "Please don't apologize. We sure want to talk some more in the morning after a good night's sleep." After Dan and Sue were nice and warm in their sleeping bags, they prayed and asked the Lord to help them lead Jake to Jesus.

The next morning, Jake invited Dan and Sue into the house for breakfast, and with the morning chill in the air, they gladly accepted. Sue volunteered to make the eggs, bacon, and toast. Jake was happy to let her so he and Dan could talk about fishing. After the meal, they were still sitting at the table when Sue looked at Jake and asked if he knew anything about God. He said, "Yeah, he's a good cuss word, and he's in charge of everything. I guess people use his name in anger all the time because they don't like the way he is running things and that is their way of letting him know. Personally, I have had enough trouble in my life, and if he's the one dishing it out, I want to stay as far away as possible so he doesn't notice me and dish out more grief."

Sue said to Jake, "May I tell you a couple of little stories?"

"Sure," he said.

"There was this father that had two children, and he was the perfect dad. He taught them, spent lots of time with them, and gave them everything so they would never lack for anything. Would you believe they dishonored their father, turned their back on him, and said through their actions that he wasn't good enough for them?" Jake was shocked and asked if that was a true story. Sue answered sadly that it was and that she had another story.

"One day this guy showed up in this town. He made a few friends and started a nonprofit organization to help people. Quite often people that get help—especially when on one else could or would—are inclined to be very generous to the one that reached out to them. Anyway, this man ended up with so much money that he had to appoint a treasurer. The treasurer's job was to take anything above general and travel expenses and use it to help people. Wherever they traveled, the plan was always the same. This all sounds so wonderful and you would think he would have been welcomed everywhere he went. Sadly, that was not the case. He was hated by big crowds of people wherever he went. You have to ask yourself, why people would hate someone that came to their town with only one plan and one purpose—to help people. You will not believe this, but even some of the people that worked with him turned on him. Wherever he went, there was always a group of people that tried to dig up some dirt on him, and when they couldn't find dirt, they started telling lies. They wanted to see him dead, and eventually they did."

Jake responded by saying "I lived my life, and I did some things I know are wrong, and I am paying for them, but it doesn't look like this guy deserved anything he got." Sue asked Jake if he had any idea who she was talking about. Jake said, "No, but I sure would have liked to meet them, especially when I was younger."

Dan jumped up in excitement and said, "You can meet them now; let us introduce you. The first one is God the Father, and this story was told in Genesis 1, 2, and 3."

Jake wanted to read it for himself, so Sue handed him the Bible and she and Dan waited while he read. When he was done, he looked up and said, "Everything you said and more is right here. God looks to be a wonderful, loving father."

Dan then said, "The second one is God the Son, and his name is Jesus. The first four books of the New Testament are an account of his birth, ministry, and his horrible death at the hands of men that hated him. His entire ministry was doing good and healing all that were oppressed by the Devil. He also said, 'When you see me, you have seen the Father.' You can go over all four accounts and see that Jesus never put sickness or hardship on anyone. All he did was offer change, to improve people's lives for the better. You will see he did say some things that sound kind of harsh, but it was always the truth, and it was said only to help people get on the right track. There is much more to tell, including the ministry of the Holy Spirit and the enemy Satan, but let's discuss what we have shared so far."

Jake said he was surprised by all this and asked how come it is kept such a secret. "Why aren't people shouting this from the rooftops and on every corner?" Sue answered, saying, "You have a great point. That is where Satan comes into the picture. Remember reading about Adam and Eve and what a perfect life they had? Yet they let the Devil talk them into doubting God. Jesus showed people how to overcome the enemy by using the Word of God. That is why the Devil has worked at getting the Bible out of government, schools, homes, and even churches. Once people have no weapon, they become very easy targets. God says our tongue is an unruly evil, but it can be tamed with the Bible to bring blessings. Satan has convinced people that if something nice happens it is good luck and if something bad happens it is God. These are the two sides; God's requires faith to bring blessings, and Satan's side requires fear to bring disaster."

"I know this is a lot to take in, and we are fairly new Christians. What we do know for sure is that God's love is real and is for anyone and everyone that wants it. You can repent of your sins and invite Jesus into your life." Jake said he wanted to right away, so they helped him in a prayer.

"Jesus, I come to you a broken man, and I want you to fix me. I repent of my sins; I am really sorry. Please come into my life and be my Lord and Savior." Jake's tears trickled down at first, and then they flooded. They were tears of joy, and he said, "I didn't see Jesus, but I met him, and he really is real and loves me."

Dan and Sue left so Jake could spend some special time with Jesus. They took a little walk and found the lake. Along the shoreline the leaves on the trees had bright reds, yellows, and orange mixtures. It was a breathtaking sight. They sat down on the bank and started to praise the Lord for giving them such a wonderful assignment. They prayed for a while and then headed back to the house.

They walked in to find Jake reading the Bible. He looked up and said, "I never knew such peace was available. It's like God just gave me a bath in his love."

Sue said, "When you read through the Bible, you will see God offers lots of different blessings, but they only come with trust and acceptance.

You will read about Abraham, King David, and others that God blessed and made rich. Don't think of rich as just money. When a person receives God's forgiveness, love, peace, joy, etc., they are very rich. The reasons God wants us financially rich are to enjoy all he has created and to be a blessing to others. There was Job, who God had made the wealthiest man in the east. When he became fearful and disobedient, he lost everything, but when he repented and forgave his friends, he got back on track with God. He was forgiven and was doubly blessed. Now there is an enemy that is sneaky and tries to keep himself hidden. He does everything he can to keep God out of our life, and we literally have to battle Satan to keep God in. Adam and Eve were the first two that didn't fight for their relationship with God, and they lost what they had."

Dan asked Jake if he wanted them to leave, because they didn't want to overstay their welcome and they had accomplished God's assignment. Jake wanted them to stay and fish Lake Alto together and tell him more about his new friend, Jesus. So after lunch, a Bible study, and a prayer for catching fish, they headed down to the lake. Jake told them he usually caught just enough for a meal, but this time of the year he liked to freeze some for the winter. They each used different baits and methods, and God blessed them with a smorgasbord. They caught walleye, bass, perch, crappie, and some beautiful sunfish.

After scaling and cleaning, they had a wonderful fish dinner, and then the guys made another bonfire to sit around while talking. Jake wanted to hear how Dan and Sue came to the Lord, and they tried to give him a condensed version. Then they told him about their study at church about unconditional love and forgiveness with no exceptions. "God gives great promises if we apply this to our parents," said Dan.

Jake butted in, saying, "No way! God must know what I went through; he can't expect me to. I can't even say it."

"Do you remember when we told you earlier that Satan will do anything to keep God out of your life? This is a time to fight back with both barrels, one called love and the other called forgiveness," said Dan.

"Do you know what God did for you today? He threw your sins into the sea of forgetfulness to remember them no more. But he wants us to do the same for others, including our parents."

Jake just shook his head and said, "Hardly a day goes by that I don't think about the horrible things done to me and the things I have done.

What can I do? I don't want to get God in my life and then be rebellious right away."

Sue admitted that she and Dan were still struggling in this area themselves. "We know one thing," she said. "We can't do this on our own."

Dan asked if there were any churches in the area that the three of them could go to in the morning. He knew Jake could use some Christian friends and encouragement. Jake said that there was a couple he drove by occasionally. He told them he didn't remember ever setting foot in a church in his life, but he was willing to go.

The next morning, after breakfast, the group headed out to take Jake to his first church service. They pulled into the parking lot of the first one they came to, and it seemed as though it was where the Lord wanted them to go. There was a greeter at the door, and when they got inside, there were lots of surprised and shocked looks when the congregants saw Jake. With each and every hug or handshake, he let them know he had Jesus in his life. The praise and worship was lively and Jake didn't seem to have much trouble joining in. Afterward, the pastor came up to the podium and announced he had had a sermon all prepared, but that morning God had directed him to speak on the importance of obeying the fourth commandment. Jake, Dan, and Sue almost slid off their pew. Their surprised looks did not go unnoticed by the pastor, who now understood why God had taken him in this direction. He started out with, "In all my years of talking and counseling people, I have found very few that use words and actions that show they love and honor their mother and father. There are lots of complaints and horrible stories to justify disobeying God."

"First off, you have to understand that God works by seed time and harvest, and he thinks abundance. Our lives are seeds. The words we speak and our actions produce a crop in our life, all according to what we plant. There are people that believe God is in control and running things right down to when and how we die. It rids them of responsibility, which frees them up to say and do things they wouldn't do if they knew the truth. We choose life and we choose death. There are lots of references to our tongue; God says it is evil and has to be tamed. We eat the fruit of our lips, which determines blessings or curses. If your life is going downhill, this is not to condemn you, but for you to see you can change things through the love and power of God.

"I just wanted to set the groundwork so you see the bigness of how God set this whole system up, right from the beginning. Each human being is a product of one father and one mother, and God made an across-the-board, no exceptions commandment to love and honor them. This commandment has absolutely nothing to do with what your parents are or were like; it is only about obeying God. Why is obeying God so important? Very simple—obedience brings blessings; disobedience brings curses. For you, me, or anyone, it always is for our own good to obey God. Now listen closely. When you look in the mirror and ask, "Who is that?" you are looking at a reflection of your mother and father. You are your parents' fruit; you are a product of them. Here you have to remember that seeds produce after their kind. Many may say 'I am not like my parents; I would never do what they did.' If children were not like their parents, but much better, that would make each generation kinder and more loving than the last. Look around at this world and you will know that is not true—but it could be if people obeyed God.

"This all comes down to one thing: if you don't like who you came from, you are not going to like you. Seeds produce after their kind. You can't get a beautiful lawn out of crabgrass. It may look nice from a distance, but close-up you can see the ugly, and that is all it will keep producing. Once you commit to seeing your father and mother as beautiful, you will become beautiful. That opens up God's promises in Deuteronomy 5: 16: 'Honor thy Father and thy Mother, as the Lord thy God hath commanded thee: that thy days may be prolonged, and that it may go well with thee, in the land which the Lord thy God giveth thee.' Take a good look at the promises of blessings God offers. You may say you can clearly remember the things that were done to you and they are the facts. Your sins are also the facts. When God forgives, he doesn't remember them at all. Gone, wiped out. On our own we can never ever erase facts, but through the power of God we can—if we are willing.

"These are some of the arguments people have and hold onto: 'I never saw my real parents; I was adopted.' 'They abandoned me and left me to live a life of horror.' 'I was beaten so badly I have been permanently disabled.' On an on the reasons go, and they are sad, but don't let them control your life forever. If you can find your parents, you need to go and take them the love of Jesus, which resides in you. If they passed or you can't find them, you need to love them in your thoughts and in your heart. Today is the day of decisions. Will you come forward and pray and tell the Lord that from this moment forward, you commit to loving and honoring your mother and father? Your thoughts will be only of love, and anything else you will cast down. For those of you that say you can't do this, let me ask you a question: do you remember everything or anything you did a month ago today? What did you eat, who did you talk to, what were you thinking about, what was the weather like? See, you are capable of forgetting.

"Once you commit to obeying God, you will start experiencing his benefits. When people apply for a job, they always want to know what the benefits are. The power to do this job comes from God; you just have to obey and then enjoy his benefits. No matter how late you are, today is the day. Right now, anyone who knows their heart isn't one hundred percent right toward their parents, come forward, and we will pray together."

The pastor was not surprised to see almost everyone standing in front of him. "Once we pray, you will still have a battle on your hands. The battle will be in your mind, because old thoughts have a way of resurfacing, but you have to do what Jesus did and don't entertain evil but speak the word of God: 'It is written, and I will obey; I love and honor my father and mother, and it is well with me, and I will enjoy a long life.'

"Okay everyone, repeat this prayer. 'Father God, I humble myself before you. Thank you for your love and for giving me a chance to change my life forever. I acknowledge your orders are just, pure, and for my benefit. I will look at how you love me, and that is how I will love my parents. I will never think or speak evil of them again. They will forever be beautiful in my sight, which makes me a beautiful person. Lord, I want to thank you for my two wonderful parents. I will never judge them again. Thank you, God, that you give me the strength to do this every day for the rest of my life."

There were lots of smiles with tears coming through them. Some testified about a hundred-pound weight they had carried around now being gone. Jake said, "Love, love, love! I have never done it in my life, but it feels really good, and I am free for the first time."

Sue also spoke, saying, "I found a new kind of peace that is just amazing, and I will always see two wonderful parents when I look in the mirror."

After all the testimonies, the pastor said, "God just did a great and mighty work in your life. Do not throw it away, and always keep a thankful and loving heart."

When the service was over, Dan and Sue went back to Jake's for lunch and interesting conversation. Before leaving, Dan and Sue made tentative plans of coming back during the winter for ice fishing. All the way home, they talked about their fabulous weekend. It sure was a journey full of surprises. They arrived home, unpacked, and then visited their neighbors to pick up George and share a condensed version of their weekend with them. The neighbors were looking forward to going with them to the next fourth-commandment service at church.

# Chapter Thirteen

On Monday morning, Sue decided to try to locate her father. She didn't know where to begin, so she prayed and asked the Lord. She couldn't ask her mother, and she didn't have the addresses or phone numbers of anyone on that side of her family. It was God that's teaching her how to love her dad, and he would also show her how to contact him. Two days later, Sue was looking through her mail and spotted what looked like junk mail which she usually throws away. She felt compelled to open it and on the top were big bold letters reading, "Who Are You Looking For?" She called right away and with the information she had, they told her it shouldn't take more than a couple of days. She left right away to go to their office and pay the fee so they could get started. By the next morning, she had her father's phone number in her shaking hand. She wasn't quite ready yet and wanted to talk everything over with Dan first.

It seemed like a long afternoon, Sue accomplished a lot. She washed clothes and cleaned out closets. Everywhere she went, she said aloud, "I love and honor my mother and father, and thank you, Lord; it is well with me." By the time Dan came home from work, she not only was feeling comfortable with the words, but she realized that real love was developing as well. Over dinner she asked Dan, "When I call my dad, would you be willing to go with me to see him?"

"I will be there every step of the way," Dan said. "We have washed our parents in the blood of Jesus, so whatever may have happened in the past is gone. They have a clean slate, and our love for them is pure. Now I want to ask you what you think about inviting my parents over for Thanksgiving."

"That is a great idea. Do you realize we may have to do three Thanksgivings: my dad, my mom and Bill, and your parents?"

"That would be great; love is an action word, and this would be a great way to activate it."

After supper, Dan called his parents, and right off the bat told them he loved them very much. His father replied by saying, "Your mother and I love you, and we were just talking about how great it would be to see you and Sue during the holidays." That made it easy for Dan to invite them for Thanksgiving dinner. When all the arrangements were made, Dan hung up. He danced a little jig and said, "God is so awesome! My inside is feeling good, and I already sense the wellness God promised."

Now it was Sue's turn. Her hand trembled while she dialed her dad's number and the phone rang. It kept ringing, and Sue was just about to hang up when a familiar voice hesitantly answered: "Hello."

"Hi, Dad, this is Sue, and I just called to tell you I love you." There was dead silence on the other end, and then she head sobbing, so she waited. After what seemed like hours, her dad told her he loved her too. That brought Sue to tears. Between all the crying, the plans were made for her and Dan to go see him on Saturday.

Two calls were done and there was one to go—Sue's mom and Bill. With the first ones having gone so well, Sue had high hopes for this one. But her hands still shook as she dialed. Her mom answered, and Sue said, "Hi, Mom. Just called to tell you I love you very much."

Her mother replied by saying, "I can't talk right now," and she hung up.

Sue was floored; this was not what she had expected. "Dan, now what do I do?"

"Why not wait until our next meeting and we will talk to Pastor John. I think two out of three victories is still reason to celebrate."

All week they reminded themselves and each other to keep the new thoughts and not allow any old ones to creep in. *If the brakes on a car aren't working and you get new ones, there is no purpose to carrying the old ones around,* Sue thought. *Our lives weren't working, and God gave us a new way of living, so we have no need or desire to carry the old life around.*

On Thursday, a letter from Jake arrived, and they were hoping for good news. Sue waited for Dan to come home so they could read it together. The letter said that he was doing better than he ever believed possible and thanked us for coming and leading him to Jesus. He had decided to search for his parents and had gotten a very big surprise: they both had the same address and didn't live that far from him. He was hopeful that they might be back together. That was it. He didn't say if he had contacted them or anything about his kids. Dan and Sue would just have to wait and see. He did ask if they had any news, but they decided to wait and write him after Sue had seen her dad.

With supper and cleanup done, they decided to work on what was taking place in their lives. They knew that when God taught them something, they needed to practice it until it became natural. They had never realized how much they used to practice what the Devil told them and taught them; they found it had changed their lives for the worse, even though they didn't know what he was doing.

Now let the fun begin! Dan spoke first. "Hey Sue, I love and honor my father and mother; I have the two best parents in the whole world."

Sue answered: "That's nice, Dan, but I have to disagree just a little. I love and honor my father and mother, and I have the two best parents in the whole world."

Dan said, "We have the four best parents in the world. Do you know how we can say that?"

"Yes I do. We used to believe that the facts are the facts and there is no way to change them. Like the fact that we had sinned and were going to hell. But Jesus washed away those facts in his blood. **Love is more powerful than any fact!** We no longer justify and protect our right to suffer. Now we know God's ways are higher than ours, and he will teach them to us. Best of all, they come with great benefits. We know love has to be worked at and fought for in any relationship; otherwise, bitterness, anger, and even hate can creep in and destroy."

After all their practice, Dan and Sue were excited to be on their way to the next meeting along with their neighbors. Pastor John began by saying, "I am going to give you your biggest weapon to use before, during, and after you commit to obedience. God would not order you to do something that was impossible to do, because everything he commands is possible— even loving and honoring your father and mother.

God started things with a picture in his head, created it with his words, and said it was good. With our parents, we picture love in our heads, create it with our words, and say love is good. Loving your parents is more for your good than theirs. The only person you live with 24/7 is you, and what you choose to think about makes your day. If you want to be at peace, you have to plant peaceful and loving crops.

"Think of your mind as life's road map; what you put into it and think about is the direction your life will take. You also have to be able to decipher the terrain of that map. There are land mines, sinkholes, and traps waiting for you, all set up by Satan. The Bible is needed to instruct us to locate and disarm them. The manual is in code, so we need the author to walk us through, step-by-step. If you have never been born again, now is a great time to invite Jesus to be your Lord and Savior. If you have never done this, then today is the day. If you really want Jesus, just pray this prayer: 'Jesus, I believe you died on the cross and rose for me. I repent of my sins and need you desperately. I receive you, which gives me a brand-new life. I commit to studying your word, which will teach me how to live for you. Thank you, Jesus.'

"We are going to talk about a giant sinkhole, and that is to disobey God by not loving and honoring your father and mother. Now I have to ask you, if God commanded it and thought it was so important that he added great promises to it, how could anybody think it is okay to disobey God?

You may say you were adopted and they are the only Mother and Father you have known. Doesn't loving and honoring them count? Yes it does and you should be very grateful for what they did. But when you look in the mirror you're ultimately the seed of just one Mother and one Father. They have a big influence on you even if you have never seen them. Loving and honoring them brings so many good things to their seed, which is you.

"Now I have made everything clear. By choice, you can love and honor your father and mother. It's by choice that you wash them in the blood of Jesus and throw their sins in the sea of forgetfulness and remember them *no more*. This is what we are to think on: whatsoever things are lovely and of a good report, think on these things. To do this, you have to renew your mind with the word of God.

"If there are any questions before we pray, please ask; I will wait a moment." There was a silent pause. "Okay, everyone that is willing to commit to loving and honoring their father and mother, come forward and we will pray together."

People began getting up all over and going forward. When Dan and Sue's neighbors got up, Dan and Sue followed right behind. Even though they had already prayed, they felt they needed to keep that commitment fresh and alive inside of them. The pastor led the prayer. "Father God, I know you are kind and loving. I realize your commandments are for my benefit to obey. I do and will love and honor my father and mother all the days of my life. My thoughts and words about them will be honoring and loving. Whatever they did in the past is washed away in my mind and in my heart, and I will remember those things no more. What I will remember is to owe them nothing but love. Amen."

As people went back to their seats, there were lots of tears, smiles, and excitement. Pastor John finished the meeting by saying, "You healed your mind today, and don't you let it become sick again. If your parents are deceased, then bring lots of love and honor to their memory. We are going to have one more meeting on this in January. It will be a time of praise reports. I believe many of you will unite or reunite with your parents in a brand-new, loving way. When you see them, the only thing you are taking with you is love, and love never fails. This will be such an adventure that you probably won't even notice the benefits. Then one day it will dawn on you: 'It is well with me. I look in the mirror and like who I see. No longer will I speak evil about my parents and then about myself. I am the fruit of two wonderful people.

# Chapter Fourteen

It was a picture-perfect Saturday with a beautiful blue sky full of fluffy little clouds that looked like you could just lie on them and doze off and forget the challenges ahead. Sue was shaky on the inside, and it was showing on the outside, so Dan suggested they stop for breakfast. They did, but neither one tasted what they ate. Back on the road, Sue broke the silence and said, "You know, Dan, if this had just been preached to us once, I think I could have ignored it or buried it in the back of my subconscious. I sure hope Pastor John does this with other things in the Bible."

"Yes, it is sure different to listen and take action than to hear and forget." All this talk was to avoid discussing the face-to-face meeting with Sue's dad. They prayed during part of the trip, and when they arrived, Sue rehearsed some things before she got out of the car. First she pictured Jesus in excruciating pain as he said, "Father; forgive them for they know not what they do." He looked with love at the people that had spit on him, tried to push him off a cliff, told all kinds of lies about him, and just plain hated him for no reason. Holding back the tears, she said, "I'm ready; let's go love my father."

Sue's father must have been watching for them, because he opened the door before they had a chance to ring the bell. They entered, and Sue and her dad faced each other for a moment, and then, simultaneously, their arms reached out and they gave each other a big hug. He told them to come in and offered coffee, which they both gladly accepted. Sue introduced her husband, and there was some small talk. Then Sue told her dad there had recently been some major changes in their lives. "That is what made me realize I needed to find you and tell you how much I love you."

Her dad said, "I have had some changes in my life recently too." Sue was thinking maybe he had remarried or gotten a new job, but she was very surprised at what she heard when she inquired. He said, "It all started about three months ago. Every day on my way to work, along the same route I have taken for years, I go past this church. The only way I can describe it is to say that it seemed like it was calling me. I have never been one to get into all that religious stuff. I had always felt that if you believe in God and try to be a good person, everything will work out in the end. But I had never really thought about the end. Well, the calling got so loud I literally went into the parking lot and stopped the car and yelled at the church, saying, 'Quit calling me; I am not coming!' I guess I was really noisy, because I got some strange looks from some people walking by with their dogs. They stopped, watching for their dogs to do their duty, but I think they were really waiting to see if I was going to yell at the church again.

"I thought I had won, because on the way home there was nothing. I was kind of smug in my attitude that this church wasn't going to tell me what to do. My little reprieve didn't last long. The next morning, it was louder than ever. I pulled over and put my hands over my ears and said quietly, yet forcefully, "I am not coming." On the way home, I decided to risk getting a ticket and was speeding past the church. It was not a good plan, because I did get pulled over. What was I going to tell the officer—'I had to get on the other side of this church in a hurry so it wouldn't talk to me'? I just took my ticket, which made me even angrier at this talking church. The next day was Friday, and my thoughts were, 'If I just get past here two more times, then I will have the whole weekend to come up with a new strategy.'

"Friday morning I was very optimistic that I could get to work unscathed. I considered going a different direction, but I was stubborn. This was the way I always went, and I was not going to change for a talking building. That morning was the worst ever. I was two blocks away, and already I heard it calling me. So I pulled into the parking lot a broken man and said, "Okay, you got me. I will come here Sunday, just this one time, and then you better leave me alone, or I might just take you apart brick by brick to find where your outdoor speaker is.

"I woke up Sunday and tried to talk myself out of going. But, wanting to be a man of my word, I got ready to leave. I gave a few chuckles, realizing I was putting on a suit and tie for a talking building. I wanted to make sure everything was done right, because there was not going to be a next time. As I walked in the church door, there was more handshaking and hugging than at an election campaign. I was very suspicious, thinking, 'Did they know I was coming?' When service started, I was shocked right

76

away. It sounded like happy music. My very brief memory of church was a very sedate service, and trying not to sneeze or cough, because you might make God angry. Before I realized it, my mouth was singing and enjoying it. They were songs all about a great and loving God. There were prayers and then the sermon, which was all about Jesus and what he did for us.

Somewhere along the way I melted like an ice-cream cone on a ninety-degree day. I turned into mush on the inside. The pastor made a call for anyone wanting to invite Jesus into their life to come forward to pray and meet their Lord and Savior. I moved out into the aisle and fell flat on my face. What happened was, my inside wanted to run and my outside wanted to be reserved and move slowly. The two met head-on, and down I went. I got up right away, hoping no one noticed, and quickly walked to the front. When I prayed and invited Jesus into my life, I turned into a bowl of Jell-O and went down on my knees. Then the weeping started. It seemed like I was there a long time, and all that went on inside was "Jesus is real, Jesus is real, Jesus is real." When I got up, everyone was singing and didn't seem to even notice me, so I went back to my seat and joined in.

"On the way home I started thinking God was having a laugh or two at my stubbornness. Then I wondered why I had been so reluctant. I had fought it like I was going to the dentist to have all my teeth removed. But outside of the embarrassment I caused myself, it was wonderful. I really know God loves me and there is a connection now. In a nutshell, your dad is a Christian. Sorry it took so long to explain, but everything was important, and I couldn't leave anything out."

Sue said that she loved every word of his story and told him that she and Dan had recently become Christians and had a story too. I guess these things happen because God is not mundane but likes adventure—that must be where we get it from. How about we take you out for lunch and tell you how God lassoed and hogtied us with his love. We fought him too; I guess most people do.

During lunch they filled each other in on jobs, hobbies, and other small talk that always circled back to God. Sue's dad was still working for the same company, just a different city, and he was doing office work instead of traveling. Dan talked about his job and the many steps that led them to Jesus. "Arriving here to find out you're a Christian too is above and beyond anything we could ask or think."

The next morning before they left, Sue's dad said to Sue, "I know you came here in love and hold nothing against me no matter what. I just want to explain to you what happened. You know I loved you and tried to be a good dad, but your mom was everything. I really thought we had a good marriage, so when Bill told me she was in love with another man and that he had seen them together, it hit me like a ton of bricks, and I went off the deep end. It was an instant pain that was unbearable. I never drank, but I found myself in front of a bar and went in and got wasted. I don't even know how I made it home. I wanted to humiliate your mother, and instead I hurt you. But I am telling you the truth; I didn't realize it until the next day, and then the only thing I could do was run. I was not able to face you and still wouldn't have been able to today except for Jesus and his forgiveness. Now I want to ask for your forgiveness."

Sue said, "Of course, that was done before we came, but you don't have the whole story straight. I didn't know if I did either, but you just confirmed it. I had no plans of telling you the truth, because I was afraid of what you might do. But I know that with you having Jesus, you will be okay. I don't know if I am one hundred percent accurate, but your side was, so I believe the other side is also. This is what I surmised: Bill became obsessed with mom, and we know obsessions can drive people to do just about anything, and in many cases there is no limit. I believe mom never cheated on you. Bill convinced her that you cheated and convinced you that she cheated, which broke up your marriage. He was there to comfort her—to the point that she married him." She looked at her dad, waiting for some kind of response, but there was silence for a long time.

Sue didn't know if she had done the right thing, and she just waited while her dad processed everything. Meanwhile, negative thoughts ran through her mind like a marathon runner. "What if he explodes, what would I do? Is he going to hate me for telling him information he didn't want to hear? What if he thinks I really came here to cause him pain?"

He finally looked up and said, "I'm okay. I was in shock, so I started praying right away. I can't change the past, so God gave me two options: forgive and have his peace, or carry it and be tormented. I may be a new Christian, but I know a good deal when I see it, and I am going to forgive everyone—including myself—and have God's peace. I am glad you told me, because now I can move on with my life, and maybe someday I will even find someone and remarry."

Dan suggested taking obedience one step further and having a prayer time for Sue's mom and Bill. After the prayer, there were some good-bye hugs and tears, and Dan and Sue left for home.

# Chapter Fifteen

On Monday morning, after Dan left for work, Sue thought about her mother and Bill and asked the Lord, "What do I do next? Do I try calling again? Do I go over there? Do I write a letter? Do I just do nothing for now?" She didn't hear or sense anything, so she decided to just go shopping. She thought she might even look for a Christmas present for her dad. During all the years it was just her and Dan, she hadn't shopped for gifts. They would just decide to take some money and buy something for the house that they both wanted. She didn't know what she would get for her dad, but she was going to have fun looking.

Sue walked through the men's clothing, tool, and jewelry departments. While looking, she realized she didn't know his size, if he still worked with tools and what he might need, or if he could maybe use a new watch. She left the store empty-handed, and on the way home she went past her new favorite store, Life in the Love Lane Christian Bookstore. *Now here is the perfect place to find something for my father*, she thought.

She went in, and within a few minutes, she had found ten books she thought her dad might like. Her decision was to purchase three, write down the names of the other seven, and talk to Dan. They had an unwritten agreement that they were both free to make small purchases, but anything big they would consult each other about first.

She arrived back home and heard the phone ringing as she entered. She dropped her package and purse and ran for it, thinking it was Dan. To her surprise, it was her mother. "Sue, it's your mom. I just wanted to tell you I am sorry for hanging up on you the other day. I really was glad to hear from you. It was just that it was so unexpected I was speechless."

Sue thanked her mom for calling her back. "Dan and I would love to have you and Bill over for Thanksgiving dinner. It's time to put the past in the past and enjoy the day. Can we do that, Mom? I love you!"

"I would love that, and I will be there for sure, and I'm pretty sure Bill will come too. Have you spoken to your father?" Sue couldn't lie, so she just said yes. There was no response, so they just said their good-byes.

That evening, when Sue heard Dan's car pull into the driveway, she couldn't wait. Out of the door she ran, and she quietly began screaming, "More victory! More victory! My mom called."

Dan said, "Will you please wait until I get in the house, take off my jacket, and sit down. Then you can tell me all about it."

Sue spoke volumes, all in two sentences: "My mom called; she is coming for Thanksgiving dinner and asked if I'd talked to my dad. She didn't respond when I told her I had. It sure would be nice if we could have all four of our parents here, but that doesn't seem like a good idea with Mom being married."

On Thanksgiving afternoon, Dan's parents arrived, and shortly after, Sue's mom. She commented, "Bill didn't look so good when I left, and he seemed nervous about something."

Sue didn't say anything, but she was hoping he was feeling guilty for what he had done many years ago.

There was quite the spread of food, but before they ate, Dan and Sue said a prayer of thankfulness and also the good news of the gospel, which brought some strange looks when they said "Amen." After a nice meal and visit, the parents left. Dan and Sue thought everything had gone well.

The next morning, Sue was whizzing around the house cleaning as though she were in a hurry, but she didn't know why. She had no place to be, and making meals would be a breeze with all the leftover turkey. The phone rang just as she finished lunch. It was her mom, and she was crying. "What's wrong mom?" she asked. "Please try to calm down."

Sue's mom was working on composing herself enough to speak. When she did, she relayed some shocking news. "Bill has left me! I don't know why; we didn't have a fight. He left a strange note that made no sense. I sat looking out the window all night, thinking he'd return. I even made his favorite breakfast. I finally gave up and just kept rereading the note. "Sue asked her mom if she wanted to share it, and her mom started reading. "'My darling Barb: By now you have found out the truth and I can't face you. Everything I did was because I couldn't live without you, and I don't know if I can now. Love always, Bill.' I don't understand this at all; what did I do wrong? I just came by your place and had a nice visit. Sue, I don't know what to do."

Sue said, "You are in no condition to drive anywhere; would you like me to come over?"

"Please, if you can."

"I will get some things together, leave a note for Dan, and be on my way."

While driving, Sue felt a mixture of sad and happy thoughts. The sadness was for the pain her mother was going through. "No matter how old a child gets, that child always would like to see his or her parents together. Yesterday I couldn't even think of that possibility because Mom was married, but if Bill is truly out of the picture, it seems like something I might be able to work on."

That last thought inspired Sue to pray for her parents the rest of the way there. As she pulled into the driveway, she had no idea what to do or say, but she asked the Holy Spirit to lead her and direct her path. When her mom opened the door, she looked bedraggled and old beyond her years. After they hugged, they went into the living room and sat down, and Sue's mom gave her the note to read. Her mom asked her, "Can you make sense of that note? I can't."

Sue said, "I might be able to, but I need to ask you a question first. Remember years ago when Dad left? Did Bill have any information that he found out and gave you?"

"I don't see what that has to do with now. I can't deal with that and this right now. I thought you came to help me!"

"I'm sorry, Mom, I am just trying to get to the bottom of this for your sake, but if it is too painful, we will wait."

"I know you mean well, Sue, but what could anything that happened years ago have to do with why Bill left me?"

"Because if you read the note again, you can see he thinks you found out something he may have been hiding from you. This may have been bad enough for you to leave him, so he felt it was less painful to just leave than to face you. Did Bill ever tell you that Dad cheated on you?"

With a shocked look on her face, her mom asked, "How did you know? We both felt it was better to protect you."

"Mom, I really don't want to hurt you, but you need to know the truth. Dad never cheated on you."

"Yes he did; Bill saw them together the night he left, and they both had suitcases. Listen; your dad and I didn't even have an argument. He wouldn't just walk out on our marriage. There must have been another woman."

"Just now you verified your side of the story, and Dad already verified his side."

"What? You mean you talked to your dad about this?"

"Yes, Mom, I did, and he left you because Bill told him that he saw you romantically with another man. Mom, please try to understand; Bill had probably fallen for you while the four of you were friends. That may or may not have caused his divorce. It appears that after their breakup, it left too much time to pine for you and eventually plot to get you to marry him."

Her mom just sat there, and Sue could almost see the wheels turning in her head, trying to sort this all out and make sense of everything. She finally spoke. "Sue, this is really hard for me to believe. All these years, Bill treated me really well. We rarely fought, and if we did, he was quick to buy me flowers and candy to make up. Because he was good to me and I hated your dad, I let myself believe I loved him. Once we were married for a while, I knew it was a mistake, but I did want to give you some kind of family life, even though I sensed you didn't like Bill. I just took it as rebellion because your family was torn apart."

Her mind raced in so many directions that she finally stopped and asked Sue, "How is your dad doing?"

"He is really doing well, and he just recently became a Christian."

"Oh, he's religious now?"

"No, he has a relationship with Jesus. "How do you have a relationship with someone you can't see?"

In all religions people preform. They are taught by other people what to believe and how to act.

In Christianity God preforms. You actually see his awesome love.

"In the Bible, many people saw Jesus and the great things he did and still didn't believe. Anyone can reach out to Jesus with their mind and have nothing, but when they do it with all their heart, they will meet him. If you are willing to do that now, I would love to pray with you and introduce you to Jesus so you can know him too."

Sue's mom thought for a long time and finally responded. "You are a very good salesman because you have me believing Jesus loves me."

"Okay, Mom, I want you to close your eyes and let your heart see Jesus standing in front of you with open arms, and you just have to step into them. Repeat this simple prayer: Jesus, I am a sinner, and without you I would spend eternity in hell. I repent of my sins and ask your forgiveness. Jesus, I need you and invite you to be my Savior. I will trust you and serve you all the days of my life. Amen."

There were lots of tears and hugs going on, and finally her mom spoke. "I woke up this morning very heavy, but now I feel very light. What a great diet plan this turned out to be."

"Yes, Mom, but to keep that heavy weight off your shoulders, you have to study the Word of God and believe it, and it will work for you. It is kind of like having a job; you continue day after day, but you can't spend any of your wages until payday. You continue in the word of God, but you don't get the wages of his promises until you believe what he says with all your heart."

Suddenly Sue's mom jumped up and left the room. Sue sat there trying to figure out what was going on. She finally got up to look for her mom. As she turned the corner, she saw her coming down the hall, waving her Bible and saying, "I found it! I found it! Now I can start my job."

Sue became concerned about the way she had explained things to her mom, so she had to explain again in a different way. "Mom, mom, I need to expound on what I said so I don't confuse you. I just used the word 'job' because it makes people think of commitment. They have to get up every day and get ready for work, get there, and perform certain duties. With God and his word, it is a labor of love. We get into the Bible because we love God; we believe what God says above anything else. We do what he says because we love him. Why? Because he first loved us." Then they both started crying, and when they dried their happy tears, they looked and saw that it was after 2:00 a.m. and time to go to bed.

The next morning, after breakfast, they prayed and looked into the Word of God so Sue's mom could see for herself just what she had done the night before. After Sue packed up, they started saying their good-byes, which took about an hour. Her mom said to her, "I seem to have a new pair of eyes. I see things so totally different now than before you came yesterday."

"That is God's love at work! I am going to head home now, but call me anytime; and if you need me for anything, just let me know."

# Chapter Sixteen

S ue arrived back home in time to have lunch and figure out something
for supper. In between that, there was lots of time to think about
getting her parents back together. If Bill didn't return, that is.
When Dan arrived home from work, he seemed surprised to see Sue home
already. She informed him that the only reason she was there was that her
mom had received Jesus into her life last night, and she seemed to want to
explore their relationship, so she didn't need Sue at the moment. "I may
go in a few days to spend some more time with her. For now you and I
have lots to do."

"What might that be?" Dan asked.

"We are going to have our first Christmas together with family. Do
we do three separate Christmases? Do we do one for everybody? Are we
getting gifts? We need to plan a meal or meals that everyone would like."

Dan, still being the same sensitive guy he was in high school, suggested
three separate Christmases in order to take the time and make his parents
feel special, as well as Sue's parents. He also volunteered to help with all
the extra cooking and cleaning. "Seeing as how we already have presents
for your dad, we need to buy some for the others," said Dan.

"Wow! That is exactly what I was thinking. Great minds think
alike."

Dan was happy they both agreed and was going to leave the details up
to Sue. But Sue had another question. "How about we invite your parents
Christmas Eve and mine Christmas Day?" Dan wanted to know how
that was going to work. "Well, we could invite my mom for Christmas
breakfast and my dad for supper, or maybe, just maybe, they would come
at the same time, so we wouldn't have to get one out the door before the
other one comes."

Dan put his foot down on that idea. "Don't you get any matchmaking
ideas."

In the next couple of weeks, Sue spent time with her mom and mother-in-law to find out what to get them for Christmas and what kind of meals to prepare. Her mom seemed to be doing really well and was drawing a lot of strength from her new relationship with Jesus. She inquired if Sue had said anything about the Lord to her mother-in-law. "We just gave the salvation message when we prayed before our couple of meals together."

Three days before Christmas, Sue had all the cleaning done and went to spend time with her mom. She was going to help her shop and prepare some things ahead of time. Sue arrived in the afternoon, and they decided to go shopping and make beef stroganoff and a vegetable medley for supper together, and the next day, they would shop for Christmas.

When they got to the store, Sue came up with the wild idea of having a race. Each took one recipe, and whoever got all their items and made it back to the checkout first was the winner. Sue took the stroganoff, which would take some traveling; her mom's recipe wouldn't require a lot of moving around, but it would require searching for the nicest and freshest vegetables. The rules stated there was to be no running and no asking for help.

They raced to the produce department, where Sue picked up fresh mushrooms, and then she moved on to the meat counter for beef. As she left with the beef, she just missed a collision going into the noodle aisle. Then she was off to the dairy area, where she began to notice a few stares. While she was still moving, she explained she was having a race with her mom. That made things worse, because now she had people following her to see if she would win. A few were even cheering her on.

Meanwhile, Sue's mom had gotten all the veggies and had passed Sue on her way to find seasonings. They were drawing a crowd, and some changed over to support her mom. They felt a loyalty to her as the older underdog, and some even wanted to help her find the seasonings she needed. She informed them that she couldn't ask for help. So what they did was go ahead of her and make sure the aisles were clear. This was enough to get her to the checkout five seconds before Sue.

Among all the cheers, they left the store feeling like a couple of celebrities. They laughed on the way home like a couple of kids. It was fun to create fun memories to help make up for all the years of separation. Sue said, "I've got an idea; how about we pretend to do a cooking demonstration or show while we make lunch together?" Her mom agreed and added, "We have missed so much time together, and good memories are the best gift we can give."

When they had unpacked and everything was ready, they first had to think of a name for the cooking show. Sue said, "How about 'Easy Cooking, Delicious Eating' or 'Fresh Food Excellence'?"

"They are both good, so let's use both of them."

As preparation began, they expounded to their invisible audience on what they were endeavoring to do. As much fun as they were having, by the time it was done, they were both so hungry that it could have been bad and still would have tasted good to them.

After they had eaten, Sue asked her mother how she and Jesus were doing. She said, "Things were going pretty good, and then one evening I couldn't get to sleep, and everything that happened with Bill and your dad seemed to take over my mind, and I was not able to shake it. I got up and went into the bathroom and looked in the mirror, and I looked terrible. I started to tell myself 'Jesus loves me' over and over again. I am not kidding: all of a sudden I was glowing, peaceful, and even pretty. I went back to bed and slept like a baby."

"That is so wonderful, Mom. Jesus sure seems to bring adventure in people's lives once they start seeking him; it is amazing. I sure am glad I am staying overnight and you are helping me get ready for Christmas."

Sue awoke the next morning and didn't feel very good. She thought about it and realized it was the fourth morning in a row she hadn't felt good. She figured it must be morning flu, because once she was able to get up and active, she felt fine. She knew she couldn't be pregnant, because her female parts were so damaged after her abortion she had had a complete hysterectomy. While she lay there, she allowed herself to think about the baby she had aborted. "How did I ever think I had the right to decide whether a human being could live a full life or have none at all?" At least with God's forgiveness I know I will see him or her in heaven.

Sue's mom got up, showered, and got ready to go shopping. Sue wasn't even up, so her mom went in to wake her. "I'm sorry, Mom, I was up earlier and didn't feel good, so I went back to bed and eventually fell asleep. I feel better now."

"Dear, just think about how much God loves you, and this will pass."

"Good for you, Mom, you learn fast. Attending to something and dwelling on something are two different things."

Over breakfast they went through some cookbooks to make their shopping list. Back at home, they started preparing things they could make ahead of time, including cutout sugar cookies with lots of sprinkles. While baking, they talked about family, including Dan's parents. Sue knew she shouldn't, but she just had to ask her mom if it was okay to ask a very personal question. Her mom said that it depended on what it was. Sue said, "I was just curious, even though I know it's none of my business—do you still have feelings for dad?"

"Funny you should ask that now. I was just thinking about when your dad and I made Christmas cookies together before you were old enough to join us. We had a lot in common and enjoyed each other's company."

Sue felt her mom was avoiding the question, but it gave her some hope. Her mom would not say anything else about it. When they finished, Sue packed up everything and headed home.

That evening, when Dan and Sue took George for a walk, Sue decided to bring up her parents. Her conclusion was that they still cared for each other. The fact that Bill had filed for a divorce and her mom was no longer distraught was another indicator that there was hope for her parents. She asked Dan, "Why not have both my parents here together Christmas day? How much fighting would two people—Christians, mind you—do on the celebration day of Jesus' birth?"

Dan responded by saying, "It's not that; we know they would be fine on the outside. But how would they be feeling on the inside? Would they be able to enjoy the day? I think the real question here is, are you sticking your nose where it doesn't belong by trying to get your parents back together?"

"No, I just feel it would be better for both of them if they got back together."

When Dan didn't respond, Sue had a clue that this conversation was over.

On Christmas Eve morning, Dan got up to go to work for a half day. When he inquired if Sue was going to make his breakfast, she just moaned and said she didn't feel good. Dan became slightly suspicious and asked, "Are you sick because you want your parents here together tomorrow? Or, if you have been sick all week, don't you think you should go to the doctor? Or are you just getting lazy on me and don't want to make my breakfast anymore? I don't want you to answer; you just do whatever you need to do to help you feel better."

As soon as Dan's truck drove off, Sue felt fine and got up to make the stuffing and get the turkey ready to put in the oven. Whatever she could do about tomorrow had to be done soon. She figured she could catch her dad before he left for work, so she called him first. "Dad, I have a question for you. I haven't been feeling too good lately, and I was wondering if instead of two Christmases we could do just one."

"Are you asking if I mind if your mom and I come at the same time?"

"Yes, Dad, I am."

"Well, dear, if you haven't been feeling good and have to cook for Dan's parents today, I would think your mother and I could handle being in the same house for a few hours. Then you just have to prepare one meal, and I'm sure we could all pitch in."

"Thanks, Dad, I will get back to you, if it will work for mom."

They said their good-byes, and Sue called her mom. She played the same "I haven't been feeling good" card with her too, and she was a little more reluctant but conceded. She said, "You rest in the morning, and if you still aren't feeling good, I will cook the meal."

"Are you going to be okay seeing dad?"

"I guess I have to be; I can't expect you to always have separate holidays for us."

Sue danced into the kitchen and put the turkey in the oven, and then she talked to it through the window. "I am in a mess, and you are going to help me out. You have to give out lots of aromas when Dan comes home, and be tender and juicy when we eat. One more thing—if Dan brings up my parents, you have to call me to come baste you and take your temperature. You are my only distraction. Neither of my parents is happy about this arrangement, and Dan won't be either." Sue's strategy was to tell Dan about both her parents coming right before his parents arrived, and then by the time they left to go home, he would be calmed down.

Dan walked in the door and didn't say anything about Sue's parents. She figured he was too excited about his mother and father to think about hers. *What a break*, she thought. The next step was pretty tricky, but she guessed his parents were only a couple of blocks away. "Dan, I just wanted to tell you I am not up to making two meals tomorrow, so both of my parents are coming in the afternoon. Oh! I think your parents are here."

Dan looked out the window and said he didn't see them.

"I think they are just turning on Celery Street, so they will be here really soon. I think that is so cool that our mayor changed all the names of the streets to different fruits and vegetables to encourage everyone to eat healthier. Wasn't that a great idea dear?"

She saw a look of disdain on Dan's face, as he looked out the window and shook his head. Sue was so excited when she finally saw Dan's parents coming down the road. At least for now, she was safe with her plan. They seemed to feel much more comfortable than they had on Thanksgiving. For Dan and Sue, it didn't matter what they said or did; they had one-track minds set on loving them. They had requested turkey again, and this one was even better than the last. They liked their presents, which were Sue's idea: in a card were coupons for a father/son and a mother-in-law/daughter-in-law shopping trip. Afterward they would all meet for supper.

Dan and Sue were shocked by Dan's parents' gift to them, which were some books from the Christian bookstore, and they added that they had even bought a Bible. Dan and Sue remained cool and thanked them, but inside they were doing cartwheels and flips. Dan's parents stayed after dinner for some Dutch apple pie with warmed cream on top and to play some games. They seemed to be relaxed and in no hurry to leave. This prolonged the "do not meddle" lecture Sue was sure was coming before his parents even get out of the driveway.

After they said their good-byes and left, Sue prepared herself for Dan to start in. Whenever he would open his mouth she would think, *here it comes.* By the time they were done cleaning up and ready to go to bed, Sue was really mad. *How come when someone doesn't say what you don't want them to say but are sure they are going to say, and you keep waiting for them to say it, but nothing is said, it can make a person really mad?*

On Christmas morning, Sue woke up not feeling good again; a short time later, Sue was up and feeling better and ready to get to work. She wanted to stay on the move to continue to protect her plan. *A moving target is harder to hit,* she thought, *especially by a questioning husband.*

In the late afternoon, Sue's mom arrived first and kept looking at the door. Sue couldn't help but wonder whether she was trying to think of an excuse to go home or looking forward to seeing her former husband. She decided the best thing to do would be to keep her busy. "Mom, do you know how to make ham gravy? Mine never seems to turn out very good."

"Yes, I learned from your grandma Jo, and I would love to teach you. First preheat your oven to 325 degrees. Place the ham in a roasting pan with two inches of water. While you do that I will write down the recipe for you."

Take approx. fifteen whole cloves and some ground cloves—distribute them all over.

Put in oven at 325 degrees for one hour.

Remove ham and cover it with one can crushed pineapple and one cup brown sugar.

Put ham back in oven one to two hours, adding water if needed.

When ham is done remove from oven and put approx. 3 cups of the ham juices in a sauce pan.

Add ½ cup of flour to 1 cup of water, mix with hands so there is no lumps.

Add this to ham juices along with a ¼ to ½ teaspoon of black pepper. Add a small amount of Kitchen Bouquet. This is a browning and seasoning sauce that comes in a bottle.

Add small handfuls of brown sugar one at a time until you get just the right taste.

Continue cooking over low heat until thickens, stirring often with a whisk.

This recipe could vary somewhat according to the size of ham and the amount of gravy desired. Enjoy!!

Sue was so busy that she never heard her dad arrive. He came into the kitchen to find out what smelled so good. Sue playfully made introductions. "Dad, I would like you to meet my mom, and Mom, I would like you to meet my dad." They shook hands with fake smiles on their faces. The whole evening followed that way; every look and every word seemed to be put on just for Sue's sake. The highlights of the evening were prayer, Christmas songs, and ham gravy.

After they left, Sue lay on her bed and cried. Dan sat on the edge of the bed beside her to give her some comfort. She decided not to say anything, because that might open the door for Dan to say, "I told you so." Sue composed herself and got up to go clean up the kitchen.

The next morning, Sue woke up after Dan had left for work. She felt good physically but not so good emotionally. She had to ask herself if she really had pretended not to feel good just to get her parents together.

Even she couldn't answer that question. She talked herself into some good therapy: shopping!

Sue shopped for a new outfit for New Year's but couldn't find anything, so on the way home she stopped at the grocery store to pick up a few things. She looked around in the health and beauty department to see if there was anything like medicine for morning flu, afternoon flu, or evening flu. *How could it tell what time it is? For that matter, how come pregnant women have morning sickness? How does the body know it is morning?* Just as she was asking herself all these questions, she passed a rack of pregnancy tests. She stopped to look at them and thought: *I've never been able to take one, because I can't have children. But today I am going to pretend I am a newly married bride who has been having a queasy stomach for the last few days and wants to find out if she is pregnant.* Into the shopping cart it went—with a decision to have a little fun, because this was something she couldn't change anyway.

When Sue arrived back at home, she was hungry and almost forgot about her extra purchase. When she did finally remember, she made a big deal out of it. She first made a pretend call to a close friend that already had two children. She talked with confidence and told her she would call her right back with the results. Then into the bathroom she went, and to her surprise, the test result was positive. She laughed and called the pretend friend back with the news. They chatted about babies for a while, and then Sue hung up.

*There is no way,* she thought. *I know there is no way, so just forget about it.* She tried to count the mornings she was sick. *Come to think of it,* she thought, *my clothes are a little tighter.* Then the word of the Lord came to her, reminding her that all things are possible to those that believe. *But Lord, I never even thought about this, let alone believed it could happen. Oh, wait a minute. Back when I first started to work on obeying God by honoring my mother and father, I did have a brief thought of how wonderful it would be if I could give them a grandchild. Okay, the first thing on the list is to go and get another test before Dan comes home, because if this is somehow true, we need to share the moment together.* All the way to the store, her hands were shaking, and she tried not to get to happy, but she was getting happier by the minute, just thinking of the possibility. She grabbed a test and started toward the door, and then she remembered she had better pay for it first. All the way home she tried to pray, but she didn't know what to say. She started supper immediately when she walked in the door, so it would be ready as soon as Dan arrived home. Her mind was going wild with the possibility that she could be pregnant. She decided that if she wasn't, it would at least be nice to have this little bit of time to be excited and even think about names.

*How do I handle things with Dan?* She wondered. *What happens if I give him hope and then there is no baby? Or what if there is and I don't tell him?* She decided she had to tell him and face the results with him. They could always adopt, now that they have a family to give a baby.

As soon as Dan walked in the door, Sue told him supper was ready. He said, "What's the hurry? Is it okay if I take off my jacket and wash up first?"

"Of course, dear; I was just letting you know you don't have to wait as usual."

When they did sit down, Sue finished fast and was cleaning up before Dan was even half done. He asked if they had to be somewhere he had forgotten about. "No, dear," said Sue, "I just want to talk to you."

"Tell me you're not planning to invite both your parents together for New Year's? Remember that Christmas did not go well for either one."

"I haven't talked to either of my parents today; this pertains to just you and me, for now."

Dan was getting curious, especially when she put 'for now' at the end of her sentence. He hurried and finished his supper; he didn't take a second helping even though he was still hungry. Sue watched him take his last bite and led him into the den immediately.

She grabbed her Bible, sat down next to Dan, and began reading in Genesis 18. "And he said, I will certainly return unto thee according to the time of life, and, lo, Sarah thy wife shall have a son. And Sarah heard it in the tent door, which was behind him. Now Abraham and Sarah were old and well stricken in age: and it ceased to be with Sarah after the manner of women. Therefore Sarah laughed within herself, saying, after I am waxed old shall I have pleasure, my lord being old also? And the Lord said unto Abraham, Wherefore did Sarah laugh, saying, shall I of a surety bear a child, which am old? Is anything too hard for the Lord?'"

"Oh," said Dan. "You rushed through supper to have a Bible study; that's wonderful. Are you going to continue the story?"

"Not right now; I have something to do." She took the pregnancy test out of the bag.

Dan looked at it and said, "You? I mean us?"

"I think so, but let's see what this test says."

It came out positive. Dan looked at Sue and asked, "Are we going to have an impossible baby like Abraham and Sarah did?"

"It looks that way. That is why I hurried you through supper, because if it was positive, I wanted to call the doctor's office before it closed to get an appointment. Let me go do that right away."

Sue returned with the announcement that there was an opening the following morning at 9:00. Dan said, "I am going with you. If you really are going to have a baby, we are going to celebrate all day long, and if not we will still spend the day together and maybe discuss adoption."

Sue woke up feeling sick and decided that was why there was an early morning appointment available. She didn't care, because all she had to do was manage to get dressed, and Dan would warm up the car and drive her there. Upon arriving, Sue was given some paperwork to fill out, with lots of questions. She didn't write down anything about the fact that she couldn't have any children. Sue didn't know that the doctor would have her records sent over.

When Sue was called to an exam room, the doctor asked her what she was doing there. "According to your records, you had a complete hysterectomy."

"I know that, but I have had all the symptoms and even took the test twice." "Have you ever heard of false pregnancies?"

"Yes, but I believe this is a real baby."

"Okay, just for your peace of mind I will examine you, and we will see."

Afterward the doctor reported that even doctors make mistakes. "My report tells me you are pregnant, but I want you to see another doctor, because you can't be. I will call and see if he can see you right away."

Dan and Sue left to drive to the other side of town with the report to see another doctor. Sue said, "I am beginning to feel more and more pregnant by the minute. When God does something, doctors can be baffled."

Dan said, "I know all things are possible with God, but I have to admit I am a little baffled too. If we really are going to have a baby, I am going to have to start calling you Sarah."

"I am not ninety years old, and I am not going to laugh at God—and you better not either."

"At least Sarah still had her equipment; you have nothing—or should I say you had nothing."

Sue was glad she was seeing another doctor. *It will be so much fun listening to him*, she thought. *He'll be trying to deny something he knows is true, but in his mind is impossible.* "Here we are," she said. "Let's go and get another report."

They walked into the waiting room, and Sue felt right at home with all the other pregnant women; only she wasn't showing, and they definitely were. There was a long wait, and when they were finally led to the examining room and the doctor came in, Sue felt an instant connection. The doctor said, "I received the report from the other doctor that you are going to have a baby, but the report also says you can't. There is only one explanation, and that is—you are having a miracle baby. Seeing as you are here, we will check you again, but it is actually too early to be one hundred percent positive. Afterward the doctor told them he was as close to sure they were having a baby as he could be. "We have to treat you as though you are pregnant. My nurse will give you a list of dos and don'ts and a prescription for vitamins. Stay away from stress; get lots of exercise, like walking; and I will see you in a month." Dan and Sue were very excited to make the follow-up appointment, and they smiled at the other women as they left.

"Are we going to go somewhere and celebrate, or does the little mommy want to just go home and rest?" Dan asked.

"What I really want to do is go get something healthy for the two of us to eat, and of course you too, and then go to some stores and look at baby clothes."

"Okay, Sarah, your wish is my command."

"I will remember you said that, and you can be sure I will not try to stop you from spoiling me, my lord Abraham."

The restaurant they went to was very busy for so late in the morning, and Dan and Sue decided to have some fun. After the waitress took their order, they started in. "My dear husband Abraham, has the Lord spoken to you lately?"

"Why yes, Sarah, he has. Might you be interested in what he said?"

She laughed and asked, "Is he still telling you that you are the father of many nations? He has a big sense of humor to tell a man almost one hundred years old that he is going to have a baby. Did God forget I am barren?"

"No, dear, you are going to have a baby even though you can't."

"That's absolutely absurd, Abraham, have you gone off the deep end?"

Sue noticed people at the tables around them had quit talking and were listening, probably wondering if there was or wasn't going to be a baby. Then Dan continued. "Sarah, dear, the Lord was not pleased with your laughter; remember, there is nothing too difficult for God. Do you know why God has picked us?"

"No dear, why?" Everyone in the restaurant was waiting for the answer.

"The reason is that we will command our children to keep the way of the Lord."

"Okay, my master Abraham, I will have your son and not laugh about it anymore. Please tell me you won't punish me for my doubting."

"No, I will have mercy on you, for though I am you master, you are my queen."

After finishing the meal, they paid the bill; and as they walked out, they felt many pairs of eyes on them.

Then the shopping started. After an hour, Sue could tell Dan was tiring of looking at baby outfits, but she could also tell he was still enjoying it. On the way home, they stopped and picked up Sue's vitamins and some healthy foods. "This little one is going to be used to fruits and vegetables by the time he arrives."

"What makes you think it's a boy?" Dan asked.

"Well, that is what Sarah gave Abraham, but one of each would be nice too." After a look from Dan that Sue couldn't figure out, she added, "One would be just fine. What I was really thinking was that we should let the soon-to-be grandparents know. How about mine on New Year's Eve and yours on New Year's Day?"

"You just want to get your folks back together, and you will do anything to get your way. I have to admit having a baby looks to improve your chances.

This time I can't say no. Once they get the news, I think they will try harder to get along. Just as long as they both know the other is coming and they're okay with it."

"Yes, dear, I wouldn't do it any other way. I will call mom first, and then dad as soon as he gets home from work. If she says yes, she will still have time to back out before I call dad."

Dan shook his head and said, "Boy, you have all the strategies worked out, don't you?"

"What can I say; we women are natural born matchmakers."

"I think I don't want to hear this phone call, so I am going to take George for a walk and fill him in on today's great event."

Sue put the groceries away, took her vitamins, and got on the phone. "Hi, Mom, how are you doing?"

"Fine, dear; are you calling about New Year's Eve?"

"Yes I am, Mom. I know things didn't go very well between you and Dad on Christmas, but I really need you both here for New Year's Eve, could you do that, Mom?"

"Dear, if it means that much to you, I believe I could handle it for a few hours."

"Thanks, Mom. I will make a nice dinner, and we'll play some games and maybe go on a hayride."

*     *     *

When Dan arrived home, he asked Sue, "Well, how did the scheming go?"

"Daniel, how could you think I would scheme? I was maneuvering my words in a way that would be favorable for everybody."

"You need to work for people running for office. You could write their speeches."

"I am not going to get upset at your remark. Instead I will take that as a compliment. Did you forget we have some very important news and they need to hear it together?"

"You're right, dear; I better go call my parents. Would you like to write a speech for me, or should I just come right out and invite them?"

"Now you are pushing it; just call and ask them. I will go and write the manipulating speech I am going to make to my dad. Ha ha! I said it before you did. This is good; we want this baby coming into a home with laughter."

All afternoon, Sue stayed close to the phone. She didn't want to miss her mother's phone call in case she changed her mind and canceled. Sue didn't want to pressure her, but she knew she would if she had to. As each hour passed, she felt more confident that her mother would come even though things hadn't gone well during Christmas. "Dan, would you please come here?" she said.

"Yes, dear, what does the little mommy need, or just want?"

"Let's go through the baby name book."

"Okay, dear. A is for Adam, B is for Bob, C is for Carl."

"I'm serious, a name is very important. We want a name that says something, but not one he could easily be teased with. What about naming him after a grandparent?"

"Yes, but which one? And even if we used both names, whose would go first? We don't want this baby causing problems before he or she arrives. How about a Bible name: Peter, Thomas, or Judas?"

Sue was shocked and asked, "Why would you say Judas? No Christian names their child that. Look at all the bad things he did."

Dan started his defense speech. "That's just it; I think people only see him as bad and never look at all the good he must have done. Remember, Jesus kept Judas around but got rid of the fig tree that didn't produce. Judas had to be fulfilling his assignment. Take a look at human beings. People can do hundreds, even thousands, of things right, but if they do one serious thing wrong, they are banned, hated, kick out, and not spoken to, sometimes forever. People make life-changing decisions based on someone doing something they don't agree with. I am not talking about the one percent where people are in danger and they have to get away from someone. I am talking about the other ninety-nine times, where there is a divorce or break in a relationship because a person forgets all the good and thinks only of the bad. I am not sticking up for Judas, but what about all the good he did? Jesus sent him to preach that men should repent. He also cast out devils and anointed and healed the sick. How about Peter's claim to never deny Jesus or Thomas's need to see Jesus' scars? Today, how many people would quit going to a church once they heard stealing, lying, and doubting were going on? Jesus knew what was happening and didn't kick any of them out of his ministry. I find that very interesting, but rest assured I do not want to name our child after him."

Sue was very happy to leave the room and go call her mom back. She shuddered at the thought of having a son named Judas. He would come home from school upset because everyone was calling him a thief. "Hello Mom!" she said. "I called to fill you in on the details for News Year's Eve. How about coming around two o'clock and we can play some games, have a Bible study, and eat dinner, and I will try to make reservations for the midnight hayride. And I don't want you driving home late, so you can just spend the night; we have a couple of guest rooms."

"Does that mean your dad is staying over too?"

"I didn't even call dad yet, but it will all work out. I am just excited you are coming."

*Everything is set with my mom; now to spin the web to trap my dad,* Sue thought. She had perfect timing calling him; he had just walked in and taken his jacket off when his phone rang. She gave him the same speech she had given her mom, and she asked him if he would be okay with mom being there and told him she would like him to spend the night instead of being out on the road. He said he was glad to come and that he had been working on the past, but he still couldn't make any promises about his behavior. After Sue said her good-byes and hung up, Dan said that there could be a problem. "What if they are having so much fun they don't want to leave in the morning so we can get ready for my parents?"

"I have a super idea—why don't we just tell them the truth!"

"Watson, I think you might have something there."

"Certainly Sherlock, once they know about the baby, they will certainly understand we need to tell your parents too."

"This case is solved. Now on to the next case: what are we having for supper?"

"Oops! I was so busy planning phone calls, I forgot about preparing supper."

"That's okay, my dear; I will take you out and wine and dine you. Minus the wine, that is." "Sounds good; just let me get my coat, and I will be ready. Are we going to make a scene like we did this morning?"

"I think not. For supper, we shall be refined as we dine, unless God directs differently."

# Chapter Seventeen

The next morning, after Dan left for work, Sue filled her dining room table with cookbooks. She wanted to plan the two best meals ever. After a long hunt, it came down to a salad, crown roast, a vegetable medley, and key lime pie. I need to find something equally as great for Dan's parents. Seafood, that's it! This sounds great: jumbo shrimp with cocktail sauce, crab legs and warm butter, and scallops. I'll accompany that with parsley red potatoes, green beans with slivered almonds, squash soup with fresh chives, and for dessert a New Year's cake.

When Dan came home that evening, Sue had supper ready and was prepared to spring her menus on him when his belly was full. "Look this over; these are the menus for our parents. What do you think?"

He looked at them and said, "I think I have to go out and get a part-time job to pay for these." "It will be fine, dear; I will take it out of my happy money!"

"You're what? Don't tell me you are printing yourself counterfeit bills."

"No! Haven't you ever heard of people putting money away for a rainy day? Well, whenever I buy something on sale, I put the difference between the regular price and the sale price into an empty pickle jar. Then, when I am in a pickle and need extra for something, I am happy I have it. Thus, my happy money!"

"How come you never told me about this system?"

"You never asked, dear. I have plenty to cover the meals, and it really is a happy occasion."

"The last day of the year is here, and it is the day the cat can be let out of the bag. Our secret can finally be shared. I didn't even want to talk to anyone today, because all I wanted to do was shout 'Guess what? We're going to have a baby!'"

"Dan, how were you able to keep from telling Stan our fabulous news?"

"It wasn't easy. Even Stan noticed I was happy on top of happy and started to ask questions, but I just told him we were enjoying God's blessings."

It was time to get the card table set up and the games out, including the old standby, Monopoly. "It would be nice if they had a baby version, with little plastic diapers and formula instead of houses and motels."

"Yes, and if you got a dirty diaper card, you would have to go to jail. The games are all out, what else would you like me to do?"

"Potatoes need to be peeled and cut up."

"Why?" Dan asked. "That wasn't on the menu."

"Yes, I forgot. Some people don't think dinner is dinner if it doesn't include mashed potatoes and gravy. Everything else is ready, except we haven't discussed how and when we are going to spring the news. I think we should do it early; that way we don't have to be concerned about letting something slip. Then we can discuss and plan the baby's whole life."

At exactly 2:00, the doorbell rang. It was Sue's mom. "How did you arrive at exactly the planned time?" Sue asked her.

"It wasn't easy. I used my sundial, the farmer's almanac, the weather report, a map, and—just to make sure—prayer. Is your dad here yet?"

"No, he isn't. If he is exact as you, he will be arriving at two thirty. We wanted you to get comfortable first, and besides, I could use your help in the kitchen. Everything is set, but there is some cleanup."

"Did you put on some holiday weight, dear? I know I have. Maybe we could work out together."

"That sounds great, Mom. It is always more fun working out with someone."

There was no 2:30 arrival, and they decided Sue's dad hadn't used all the scientific sources that her mom had used. "Now I have one more brownie point than your dad," Sue's mom said.

"Sorry, Mom; I have a different system in mind. I am giving you each one hundred points to start off with, and you can both work at not losing them."

"That sounds like my daughter; you like to do things differently."

Dan chimed in. "You are right, Mom. Listen to this: Most people save for a rainy day. Well, your daughter saves happy money."

"Tell me she's not printing it; I don't want to visit her in prison."

"That's what I thought! I will let her explain."

Just then, at 2:45, the doorbell rang; it was Sue's dad. After greetings and directing him to go into the living room, Sue went to hang up his coat. As she came back down the hall, she heard loud voices. Her mom told her dad that he had lost brownie points for being late, and he threw back at her, "Let's not make this a contest for Sue's love."

When she walked in, her mom was telling her dad that she was just kidding and he shouldn't be so hard-nosed. Sue called for Dan, wondering where he was and why he wasn't stopping what was happening. He came up the stairs from the basement and had no knowledge of anything that was going on.

Before things got ugly, it was time to give their speech. "Dan and I have something to share with both of you. Please sit down on the couch together, and *no fighting*. This speech is not as famous as Abraham Lincoln's, but for us and for the both of you, it is life-changing. Our God has blessed us with the impossible. We are bringing into this world a great joy, for you, Mom, and you, Dad, and for ourselves. In less than eight months, we will have to go to the courthouse and officially change your names to Grandpa and Grandma."

They both looked at each other and then started firing questions: "What happened?" "Are you kidding us?" "Not after all these years of marriage?" "Are you sure?"

Dan stopped them to give them a simple explanation. "We couldn't have children and didn't want to adopt, because for all these years, we didn't really have a family to give a child. After we became Christians, we started to learn that to get God's blessings; you have to do what God says. Today we can say we both love and honor our mother and father, and we believe this is a direct blessing from obedience."

"That is a double blessing for us," said Sue's dad, "because we get your love and now we get to love a grandchild. I think I can speak for both of us—we are thrilled beyond belief."

"That's right, what a wonderful New Year's gift for your dad and me. That explains why you are getting a little plump around the middle."

"Mom, I was hoping you wouldn't think 'baby' and spoil our surprise. Dan and I want you both to know we will always welcome your input and advice—as long as you know we might not take it."

"I have another surprise announcement to make," said Sue.

Dan looked quizzically and said, "This is one even I don't know about. What's the surprise, dear?"

"Well, I called about the midnight hayride tonight, and there was a cancellation, so we are all set to go! We should leave here around ten thirty." They all looked at each other and then looked at Sue.

First her dad said, "Please tell me you are kidding."

Then Dan said, "There is no way you're going; did you forget you're having my baby?"

Sue's mom threw in her two cents' worth: "You can't be serious—a hayride in your delicate condition?"

Sue said, "I knew I would run into people like you, so I called Dr. Jacobson, and he told me it was fine. I can lead a normal life, just no extremes—like running a marathon race. He is on call today, so you may put him on the witness stand."

The jurors voted that a hayride was an extreme and sentenced Sue to an evening at home with the three of them waiting on her.

Dan decided that as long as she'd turned it into a court case, he would call the doctor with all the facts and see what he said. He talked extensively with Dr. Jacobson, and when he hung up the phone, he said, "Sue can go, but I am making my own conditions. Bring along a pillow and sit on my lap."

"All right Judge Doubting Thomas, I will go along with your wishes. Now, can we play cards? I vote for cribbage and would even like the judge for my partner."

After a nice meal that everyone loved, it was time to play some more games. Sue thought things were going rather well and got up to go into the kitchen to get the fresh pot of coffee. She came back to find her parents in a heated argument. She heard her dad first: "You never could play cribbage very well, and I never want you for a partner again."

"Well, that's fine with me; you couldn't even win at old maid."

"That reminds me of what you look like."

Sue was frantic at what she heard and saw. "Please, you two have to learn to get along. You sure can't act like this in front of your grandchild."

Her father spoke first and apologized for the old maid remark, adding that Sue's mom looked very nice. Sue's mom accepted the apology. Sue reminded her parents of her condition and told them she should not get upset. Her parents smiled at her, and Dan walked into the room carrying Monopoly. They played a long game, and Sue ended up winning. She didn't know if it was a setup or if she really did win, but she didn't care, because it was time to leave for the hayride.

Her parents snarled at each other as they climbed in the backseat. Sue didn't know if she should hand them boxing gloves or Bibles, or just gag them and put them in straitjackets. *It's sad,* Sue thought, *but when people get upset, sometimes they forget what God commands, or they excuse their behavior with "God wasn't talking to me; I'm perfect."*

It was a quiet and somewhat tense ride. They arrived to find lots of people there already. The hay wagon left promptly at 11:20, and was full. As they boarded the wagon, there was a light snowfall that made everything look clean and fresh. It reminded Sue of the new start she wanted for her parents, which was looking more and more unlikely. The ride was great, but with one disappointment: Sue's parents sat on each side of Sue and Dan like a couple of chaperones.

They stopped in an open field at 11:50 for everyone to get a cup of hot apple cider and be ready for the toast. The farmer and his wife had done this for enough years that they had everything down to a science. By the time everyone had been handed cider and noisemakers, it was time for the countdown. "Five, four, three, two, one!" This was one time Sue did not want Dan to kiss her, because she wanted to see if anything transpired between her parents. But Dan did kiss her, and then he looked her in the eyes and said, "Happy New Year, little mommy; I love you."

She melted a little and responded by saying, "I love you too, dear." By the time she had a chance to look, she couldn't even see her folks. She found them on the other side of the wagon and asked, "Where have you been? I have been looking all over."

"Dear, your mom and I just walked over here to give you and Dan some privacy. We didn't think you would want to neck in front of your parents."

"Dad, we weren't necking; what were you two doing?" Sue saw two blank looks which meant either "nothing" or "we're not telling." She was overwhelmed with curiosity, but she knew that if anything had happened, she would be the last to know. That just didn't seem fair. There was no way to try to trick information out of them without getting in trouble with Dan.

On New Year's morning, they all had breakfast together. The conversation was about how great everything would be in the future. Then the good-byes were said, and her parents both left. Sue looked out the window and was shocked at what she saw and heard. Her mom yelled something at her dad. He shook his fist at her and then hit his car. It appeared to cause him lots of pain. He jumped into his car, and the tires screeched as he drove off. Sue was very upset, but she had to let it go and concentrate on getting ready for Dan's parents to arrive. It was sad and funny—her parents, both Christians, couldn't even get along to welcome in the New Year, while Dan's parents, who weren't Christians, would probably be just fine.

Sue turned to see a stern look on her husband's face. "I hope you are going to be better behaved today than you were yesterday."

"What do you mean by that, *dear*?"

"Come on, *dear*; you have to admit you were quite intrusive."

"Yes, I needed to meddle, but with your parents, I don't need to. I will just be sweet, innocent, and loving."

"Good! I knew if I stuck with it long enough, I could get you trained."

"Okay, let's not fight before your parents arrive, or they will be meddling trying to get us to speak to each other. I am going to go get ready—if I have your permission, master."

"Go and make thyself beautiful, and I will go to my den and pray for my parents—if I have your permission, great queen."

"Yes you may; and by the way, I love you."

"Ditto."

Sue walked away mumbling, "Last night I didn't want romance and got it. Today I would like some, and all I get is 'Ditto.' What a moving title for a romance novel: *Ditto, Ditto, Ditto*."

Dan greeted his parents and took their coats just as Sue came out with a plate of hors d'oeuvres. They played a game of Monopoly and some Scrabble, and then it was time for dinner. Dan prayed the salvation message and thanked God for the special event coming up and for the food. During the meal, his parents didn't inquire about the special event, so Dan figured his parents had tuned him out somewhere during the salvation message.

After the meal, Sue served coffee. While Dan's parents were sitting back relaxing, Dan and Sue cleared off the table. In the kitchen, Dan said, "Can you believe that? They didn't even hear the prayer."

"Maybe it was just the smell of the food they were thinking about."

"What now?"

"How about we just sit around and talk, and whoever the Lord leads to tell them should do so."

"Okay, but they're your parents."

"Wait a minute; you share yours, and I share mine."

After some small talk, Dan decided to let the secret out. He chuckled before he got serious. "Mom, Dad, we have some serious things to discuss with you."

"Yes, son, just so long as you know we are not interested in any of that religious stuff."

"Rest assured this has nothing to do with religion. It is about someone we met. Religions are like clubs; they decide what they want to believe and not believe and then pass it on. But at some point in a person's life, they need to forget religion and come personally to Jesus, because he is the only way, truth, and life."

His dad responded by saying, "That's enough. I knew this would be about religion. We are out of here. Come on, dear."

"Okay, okay, we were just leading up to some great news, and we will just tell you. Dad, Mom, you are going to be grandparents. Sue and I are having a baby."

"You're what?"

"Yes, you are going to be grandparents."

Dan's mom looked like she was going to faint, and his dad said, "Now, son, you are not just telling us this to get us to stay so you can preach to us some more?"

"No, Dad, I wouldn't do that. Next summer, there will be a new addition to this family, and we hope you are excited."

"We are! We are!"

There were lots of hugs and congratulations. "Mom—is that okay if I call you Mom?" said Sue.

"Yes, dear; in fact, I really like it," said Dan's mom.

"Good. Then what I want to know, Mom, is, would you go with my mother and I shopping to pick out some maternity clothes soon?"

"I would love that, and of course we have to stop in the infant departments and look at all the outfits."

"Yes, we believe we are having a son, so we will look mostly at the blue outfits."

"Why do you think you are having a boy? Isn't it too early to tell?"

"It involves a story you're not ready to hear right now, so maybe some other time."

*   *   *

As the morning sun shined in the window, it tickled Sue's nose and she sneezed. She lay there enjoying the brightness, rather than the typical dreariness, of winter. Her thoughts were centered on the last two days and sorting out what had gone right and what hadn't. One thing she was pretty sure of was that this unborn baby was going to keep both sets of parents coming back. After breakfast, she decided to call her mom to try to keep things rolling. She filled her in on what had transpired the day before and how they had a challenge ahead of them.

"What do you mean 'we'; is there a plan already?"

"Of course, and this is it: You and I are going fishing in the maternity clothes department. We will find opportunities to briefly lift up the name of Jesus. He said that if he was lifted up, he would draw all men unto him. By the way, I have another plan."

"Sure you do, dear. Let's have it."

"I was thinking maybe the six of us could get together on the weekend. Then they would be outnumbered two to four."

"What six are you talking about? I think I already know."

"No, Mom, this is not about you and dad. This is only about Dan's parents. With the four of us showing them the love of God, and with the Holy Spirit directing us, it sounds like a great fishing trip to me."

"Well, you have me sold on the ideas. When do we start?"

"We are going to have fun. I will call you back as soon as I set the trap—I mean as soon as I set it up with Dan's mom. Love you, Mom."

Dan arrived home, and Sue filled him in on God's fishing expeditions. He just stood there and looked at her. Sue waited for some reply. "Well?" she finally asked.

"First off, I am going to go into the den and pray about this. I don't know if I am married to a loony or a genius."

Dan went to pray, and Sue went to the kitchen to finish supper. After about a half an hour, Dan came back and hugged his wife. "God told me that you were following him and that I should follow you. He also told me people that follow him are geniuses, because we have the mind of Christ. So what is the plan?"

106

"My mom and I thought that while we are using Bible lures with your mom, you could spend some one-on-one time with your dad and see if he will nibble on gospel bait. After supper, I will call your mom and set up a time, and then you can speak to your dad."

"What are you going to do if it doesn't work?"

"It will work. They're going to be grandparents, so they want to get in good with us. They may not be putty in our hands, but God will work it all out; we just have to obey and go."

Sue made the phone call, and her mother-in-law answered with a little skepticism in her voice. But when she found out it was just for shopping, she perked up right away with a very enthusiastic, "Yes!" She probably figured she would be safe from any sermons in a store.

Before Sue handed the phone to Dan, she whispered "Go somewhere with your dad." He nodded. "Dad, while the womenfolk are out shopping, you want to go to the sports show or bowling?"

"What about both?" he said. "You know when women go shopping; they are gone a long, long time."

"That sounds good, Dad. I will pick you up at eleven, and we can enter the fishing contest. The one that catches the least pays for lunch."

"Sounds great, and I will make sure I am really hungry, so make sure your wallet is fat."

Sue's mom arrived in time to join them for breakfast and go over their strategies. Dan said, "Okay, fishermen, let's go and throw out the bait—the love of God.

The two women picked up Sue's mother-in-law and made the usual small talk on the way to the first store. In the baby department, Barbara, Sue's mom, picked up an adorable outfit and said, "I have to get it. One day God's miracle baby is going to wear this and be so cute."

Dan's mom, Sarah, agreed and said, "Look at this one! It has a little fishing rod and reel and a tiny tackle box; I have to get it."

"Yes, fishing is such a great pastime," Sue said as she and her mom winked at each other. "Do you know who the greatest fisherman of all time was?

"No I don't; who would that be?"

"Why, that was—and still is—Jesus."

"Oh, yes, of course. Does he have any trophies?"

"He sure does; many are living with him in heaven, and they each have their very own mansion."

"Okay, you two, that's enough; I am going to go pay for my purchases."

Sue and her mom conversed and decided that was all they were going to get in for the day. They left the store laughing and decided that between the three of them they had purchased enough outfits for the first six months. At the next department store, they added a few more items. When Sue left for the fitting room to try on some maternity clothes, the two moms discussed giving Sue a baby shower around the beginning of summer. There was an exchange of phone numbers just as Sue returned.

*   *   *

Meanwhile, Dan could tell his dad was doing everything possible to avoid any talk about God. It got Dan to thinking why people are so against God, like he is a plague, when all he wants to do is love us.

"Son!" "Son!"

"Yes Dad."

"You were sure off somewhere; I have been asking you if you are ready to go fishing, so we can find out who pays for lunch."

"I am; let's go."

Dan really wanted to lose in the fishing contest so he could treat his dad, but it didn't work that way. They fished right next to each other, and Dan pulled in seven fish to his dad's one. His dad shook his head and mumbled, "I just don't get it—the same rod and reel, same bait, and same depth." Dan decided to keep his mouth shut and not tell his dad that even his fishing had improved since he met Jesus. During lunch, all was forgotten, and Dan's dad said, "At least I can still beat you at bowling."

"Okay, Dad, we will see."

*   *   *

The women, who arrived back at the house first, escorted Sue to the recliner and covered her with a blanket. Then they went into the kitchen and looked for some nice, healthy recipes in Sue's cookbooks and typed some out. Just as Barbara was going to go check on her daughter, Sarah asked, "Are you really going to get a mansion?"

"Oh Yeah! God offers first class to anyone who will become his child."

"Aren't we all God's children, and if God is first class, why is there so much poverty?" "When God created everything in the beginning it was all first class. There was no toil, poverty or sickness. That all started when Adam and Eve listened to the devil. He put just enough truth in what he told them to make them doubt what God said.

"God doesn't force anyone to be his child. He gives everyone their right to make their own choice. We chose by a decision of our heart not our head. That is a big place the devil deceives people. He convinces them that all they need to do is acknowledge that there is a God.

Dan arrived home after dropping his dad off. During supper, he compared notes with Sue and her mother. Dan said he had tried to lose at fishing and bowling and couldn't, so he had spent all his time just trying to keep his dad from getting angry at him. Then he inquired if the others had done any better. Sue said, "A little bit. We started to share Jesus in front of your mom in the department store, but she put the kibosh on that right away."

"Wait a minute; not completely," said Sue's mom. "She remembered you and me talking about living in a mansion in heaven, and she asked me about it while you were in the fitting room."

"Great! God loves to work with curiosity."

# Chapter Eighteen

Acouple of weeks went by, and Sue hadn't heard from either of the mother hens. She had talked to her dad a couple of times, but he hadn't said one word about her mom, so she decided she needed a new plan of action. Her parents didn't know it, but they had a deadline. *They need to be together before the baby is born.* She called her mom, who sounded very happy, so Sue baited her by saying, "I talked to dad a couple of days ago."

Her mom's only response was "That's nice dear."

So she tried again. "Mom, you really sound happy."

"Oh, I am!"

Still there was no information. *I sure hope raising a child isn't as frustrating as closed-mouthed parents. I guess I will just have to come right out and ask her.* "Mom, have you heard from Dad?"

"Yes, dear, we ran into each other, but I have other news."

"Wait just a minute! Back up. How? When? And where?"

"You know you are a nosy little brat. Your dad and I are adults and don't have to answer to you."

"Yes mother, but please tell me anyway."

"Okay, your dad and I ran into each other at a mutual friend's anniversary party. Are you happy now?"

"No, I want all the details. Did you talk? Did you dance? Are you going to see him again?"

"Sue, I think you need to go into the matchmaking business; then you could vent this curiosity on lots of people. Anyway, yes to all your questions."

"That's great, but now I forgot what questions I asked."

"I will tell you, and then we are going to drop it. I did talk; we both said hi, I did dance—but not with your dad—and yes, your dad and I will for sure see each other when you have the baby."

Sue didn't like what she heard, so right away, she changed the subject. "What other news do you have?"

"You know your mother-in-law and I exchanged phone numbers so we could take care of you."

"Yes, I know, and I haven't heard from either one of you. What's up with that?"

"She called me because she wanted to read about mansions herself."

"That's wonderful!"

"Yes, but that's not all. She keeps calling me and asking questions, so I have to be in the Word all the time to try to stay ahead and be able to help her. But the amazing thing is, it has been working me over like the IRS at tax time."

"That's not a very good example, Mom."

"I know, dear, but God is even more thorough and has been doing some housecleaning in my life while I have been trying to help your mother-in-law."

Sue didn't say a word, but she hoped that she would clean up the way she'd been treating her ex-husband.

After having lunch and doing some errands, Sue put supper in the oven. She had time to sit down and think about a big plan of action, which had developed in her mind by the time Dan came home from work. She told him the exciting news about his mom, which put him in a good mood to hopefully go along with her big plan. First, Sue threw out the bait.

"The big question is, now what?" Dan asked.

"Our goal is my parents back together and yours saved before the baby arrives."

Dan said, "Okay, my brainstorming mama, what have you come up with?"

"You know we haven't started to make the spare bedroom into a nursery yet, and we haven't even talked over ideas. Why don't we get our parents over here early Saturday morning, feed them breakfast, and then ask for their help. We will make sure something from each one is incorporated into the nursery. We will use everyone's talents to make it happen."

"Are you sure you want to do that, dear? Don't most mothers to be want to pick out and arrange everything themselves?"

"Normally that would be true, but remember—the main reason we didn't even want to adopt was that we didn't have an extended family to give a child to. Now that we do, I am especially thrilled to have them involved, and besides, we still have the final say on all the ideas."

"What about furniture? Did you want to buy that, or were you thinking of us men building it?"

"If there are enough carpentry skills between you, I would love to have it all homemade. We can get some magazines and books from the library, and look through them together."

Sue made the calls right away, and everyone loved the idea and could hardly wait until Saturday.

When the big day arrived, there were two big stacks of books and magazines ready to be looked at. Sue had been tempted to page through them but reminded herself that this was a family project from beginning to end. Her dad arrived first and was grinning from ear to ear for being invited to such a great event. "We feel honored to have your help, Dad," said Sue. "Shall we go in the kitchen and have tea and crumpets?"

"What are crumpets, dear?"

"I don't know, but we have some fresh fruit scones, which I can have. I have to watch what I eat, because I never know when a member of the Mother Brigade might call for a report. They have threatened to stop in unannounced and inspect the food in my refrigerator and cupboards. I guess it's their last chance to treat me like a child, because soon I will be a mom like them."

By lunchtime, the furniture, paint, and some of the accessories were picked out. After emptying a big pot of stew and a dozen rolls, they wondered if they could get up and go shopping. The men decided that not even a basketball game would keep them from the task at hand.

The wood, hardware, and stain were bought and hauled into the basement, and Dan said he sure wished it was summer so they could do this project in the garage. His father-in-law said, "Well, Dan, this is your own fault."

"You're right; I should have accepted Jesus into my life a long time ago."

They all laughed except for Dan's father, who felt he was being ganged up on.

The women arrived with a few accessories. After a brief discussion and some minor changes, the parents left, and it was set for them to come back in two weeks to begin. The guys reserved the following weekend for watching sports. Sue said, "I guess that means us wives—oops, I mean wives and friend—will get together and play some cards." Her mom shared that she had recently learned a new dice game called Farkel that was lots of fun, and she suggested they play that.

"Never heard of it, but it sure sounds strange," said Sue.

"No, dear, it is lots of fun."

Her mother-in-law said, "I am willing to learn, and maybe it will drown out some of the basketball game."

*　*　*

Sue's newest plan was in progress as her and her unsuspecting husband was on the way to meet her parents at the flea market. Sue's idea was to act tired right before lunch so Dan would have to take her home. This would leave her parents to go to lunch together. Sue was purposely late and was sure she would see her parents waiting. Step one backfired, because her mom arrived after them, and then they all waited for her dad. The two men left to go look at sports stuff, and Sue and her mom went to look for a neat antique for the baby's room. They met back at the meeting place to have lunch together. Sue claimed she was tired and needed to go home. Everyone acted very understanding and said they could do lunch another time.

On the ride home, Sue closed her eyes and imagined her parents at a nice restaurant, gazing into each other's eyes and realizing the rekindling of their love was taking place. Later they would call and thank her for getting them back together.

At home, Sue caught Dan shaking his head as they walked into the house. She knew then that she couldn't all of a sudden perk up, but had better go take a nap to avoid another lecture on meddling.

# Chapter Nineteen

The next morning there was excitement at the Frazier house. Dan and Sue prayed and discussed what they would share in church. Of course they would tell how they had learned to really love and honor their parents unconditionally. In the Word of God, they found out it is his way or the wrong way. The great thing is his love makes his way easy.

"What about Jake? He is a big part of our story," said Sue.

"What's been going on at my job is great too," said Dan, "but I think there are going to be lots of testimonies, and we need to keep ours somewhat short."

"You're right; we have to make this book we have been living into a condensed article."

Sue was so sure that after the day before, she would walk into church and see her parents sitting together, holding hands. But no, they were sitting on each side of Dan's parents. Sue wanted to pump her mom right away, so she asked her to go with her to the bathroom. Her mom reluctantly followed, knowing what was coming. "Mom, what happened yesterday after Dan and I left? Did you and Dad go for lunch together? Did you have fun? Please tell me."

"How can I answer you when you keep talking? After you left, your dad and I left separately, in separate cars."

"That's it? Didn't you at least talk?"

"Oh yeah, we did. After we said good-bye, your dad said, 'See you next week.' Now, we better get back before the service starts."

After the offering was taken, there were the announcements, one of which was exciting for the whole church. There had been three engagements between Christmas and New Year's, which was going to produce some beautiful spring and summer weddings. The pastor added that maybe there would be more engagements on Valentine's Day. "Consider this a little hint for any of you men that are dragging your feet.

"I have a sermon for this morning, but I have hopes of not having time to preach it. For those of you who are guests or new to the church, God instructed me to teach extensively on loving and honoring your mother and father, and the life-changing promises that come with it. Now we want to hear about all those results of obedience. This will prove that what God says really does work."

After an hour of testimonies that were full of love, joy, and peace, Pastor John decided to wait until the following Sunday for the rest. He pointed out that not one unkind fact had been spoken about any parent; that, he said, was the love of God. He preached a short salvation message, and some went forward to give their lives to the Lord. Dan was hoping his parents would go, but they didn't. Pastor John came and welcomed both sets of parents and invited them back next week.

On the way home, Sue's thoughts turned to her parents. She decided maybe she would just play on their sympathy. *I could act so sensitive that they would pretend to get along so I wouldn't get upset. Then one day they would look into each other's eyes and realize they didn't have to pretend anymore.* She had prepared food ahead of time, and before she realized what was happening, the men took their plates to the den to watch basketball. After cleanup, the women were talking about the nursery. This gave Sue an idea, which was to call a meeting to discuss future plans. Her mom was calling, "Sue, Sue," but Sue was deep in thought. She finally said, "Oh, Did you say something?"

"Yes, dear, we wanted to know if you are interested in playing some cribbage."

"Sure, that sounds good, but Mom, would you first go in the den and let the guys know that when they're done we should have a meeting about the nursery?

Sue's mom left and came back and said the guys agreed. Sue hoped they would say yes to her other wishes that easily. Her mind went off thinking about more plans. She would keep pursuing her goals as forcefully as the mafia and yet as gentle as a little kitten. Again, she didn't hear her mom talking to her. When she finally got her attention, she said, "For someone not at the airport, you are sure taking a lot of trips today. I would like to inquire as to where you are flying off to?"

"Sorry, I just have a lot of things on my mind—which will also be my excuse if I lose at cribbage."

At the meeting, they planned on working in the nursery the coming Saturday and going to church on Sunday. During supper, the only conversation going on was about the game and all the exciting plays. The women didn't get a word in until it was time to leave and say their good-byes.

One evening during the week, Sue sat thinking and suddenly called out to Dan, and he came running asking if she was okay.

"I thought I was," she said, "Until I started having thoughts like, 'What are we going to do if there is more than one baby?'"

Dan answered, in his great wisdom, by saying, "We will raise them."

"No, I am serious, what would we do if there are twins or maybe even triplets?"

"Well, dear, what do you think we should do? They come with no return address and no warranty."

"Don't be funny; this is serious."

"Oh, I am being serious. Our lot is big enough that if we had to add on a bedroom or two, we could do it."

"Dan, we aren't qualified to raise even one child; what will we do?"

"Calm down, dear; no one comes with a master's degree in parenting. We will let the Lord direct our paths, and we will do just fine. Now, let's not count our chickens before they hatch."

Sue laughed. "You're right, dear, but now there is something else."

"What might that be?"

"All of a sudden I have a craving for peanut butter swirl ice cream, with black olives mixed in and a can of sardines on top. Now doesn't that sound nice and healthy, and tasty too?"

"Yes, dear, I will go to the store right away and get that for you."

Upon returning home, Dan found Sue sleeping, so he put everything away quietly. Then he heard her voice from the other room: *"Where is my food?"*

"Coming, dear; I am in the kitchen."

Dan didn't want to even put the items in the same bag at the store, let alone in the same bowl. Once he had dished it out, he couldn't look at it while he walked into the bedroom. He handed it to her and said, "This must be the kind of food that turns some babies into fussy eaters." Not only did she eat it all, but she also wanted another bowl, and she offered to share this one with Dan, who quickly declined. He just hoped his stomach could hang in there to dish out another bowl.

*   *   *

Everyone arrived early on Saturday. The guys went downstairs to get started, and the mothers sent Sue on some errands while they painted. She was ordered not to come back before noon. After finishing her list, she found herself on a park bench, talking to the pigeons. She explained that she understood how it must have been for them when they were kicked out of the nest, because she was feeling the same way. She also told them about her problem trying to get her parents back together where they belonged. When Sue looked up, she saw that she had more than birds listening to her; there were some sad and sympathetic faces. Upon looking at her watch, she saw it was after one, so she excused herself and left to hurry home.

The painting was done, and wood pieces were beginning to look like furniture. They all ate lunch, and the others insisted Sue needed a nap, which she willingly took. By the time she woke up, all the parents were gone.

*   *   *

The beginning of a new week brought an old, familiar sight. *How can my parents be hearing all these sermons on love and still not even be able to sit next to each other? They must have wax buildup in their ears. But it might be a good thing; if they sat next to each other and started fighting, that could be embarrassing for all of us. Not to mention the challenge for Pastor John to break up a fight in Love in Jesus Church.* After greetings, someone tapped Dan on his shoulder; he turned around and was surprised to see Jake. There were lots of hugs and introductions. He had come to congratulate them on the baby, hear their testimony, and possibly give testimony himself. Sue and Dan were the first ones to share how they had decided to obey God, and the great results. The last one to speak was Jake. He first explained how Dan and Sue had led him to Jesus and how the pastor at the church he went too had also preached on loving and honoring your mother and father with no excuses. After really listening, he had decided to not only love and honor his parents, but also to love and honor his grandparents' memory. In doing this, he said, he found a wonderful peace and wellness he had never before believed was possible. He had made a commitment that the only answer he would give himself or anyone asking about his parents would be, "They are wonderful, and I love them. I will not let my mind go fishing to dig things up I already discarded."

After the service, Jake accepted an invitation to lunch from Dan and Sue. He gave more details on what else was going on in his life. He had been working on finding his children that he had walked out on. He knew that no one, including him, can undo what he or she has done, but he had hopes of his children forgiving him and enjoying the same wellness in their lives. So far he had located two of them, but he didn't want to make contact until he had found all four. Meanwhile, he was praying and believing God would help him make this happen.

Attending the two church services and listening to Jake seemed to be having an impact on Dan's parents. They were showing a little more acceptance and interest. Sarah was still calling Barb with Bible questions, and they were developing a nice friendship.

# Chapter Twenty

The weeks were passing quickly, the days getting longer and Sue getting bigger. She continually told her baby that she was still working on his very stubborn grandparents. At church, some friendships were developing between Sue and some of the young married women who were also having babies. Even though she was older, Sue found it fun to compare the details of pregnant life, such as cravings and letting husbands cater to needs. Sue filled them in on what was going on with her parents—actually, what was not going on with her parents. One of the women, Doreen, suggested a nice dinner with soft music. "Make some kind of dessert you need your husband to come in the kitchen and help you with," she said. "Leave the two of them at the table with a romantic candlelight setting." Sue thanked her friend for her idea and just knew it would work.

To Sue, it seemed like a wise decision not to tell Dan about the plan until it was in the making. He was extremely suspicious and seemed to have a built-in extinguisher ready to put out any of her brilliant ideas (though this one was not hers). During the week, she was able to talk both of her parents into coming for dinner Friday and then spending the night to get an early start on the nursery. The only possible hindrance would be Dan wanting to invite his parents. So Sue waited until Thursday evening and prepared one of his favorite meals of meatloaf, potatoes au gratin, and sweet corn. With Dan a little sleepy and his stomach full, Sue thought it would be the perfect time to ask. "Dear, I hope you don't mind, but I invited my parents for dinner tomorrow and to stay overnight to get an early start on the nursery Saturday. Then next week we can invite your parents."

"All right, dear," he said, and he got up and went to the den, leaving Sue in shock.

Now it was Sue's turn to become suspicious. *Either he doesn't believe my plan will work, or he just doesn't want to upset a pregnant woman. Whatever the reason, I need to think of a dessert that will take a while to prepare so I can get Dan to come in the kitchen to help me. I've got it—hot fudge banana sundaes . . . or are they called banana splits? Whatever! He can help me heat up the fudge, cut the bananas, and put it all together, which will give my parents some one-on-one time. Oh yes! I will hide the jar of hot fudge in the back of the cupboard and turn up the freezer so the ice cream is too hard to dish out right away.* The next step was to write down when to start each dish so they would all be done at the same time. *When cooking, everything is about quality food and timing. The same thing is true about matchmaking—two right people and perfect timing.*

Friday afternoon went by quickly, with Sue trying to make the dining room look warm and inviting. With all the preparations done and the food in the oven, she set the table; but she was wise enough not to put out the candles quite yet. She wanted it to look like an afterthought. *Husbands don't always understand these things, so it's best to keep them in the dark until the right moment*, she thought.

Sue's mom arrived first and commented on the fanciness of the table. "Are we expecting a celebrity?"

"In a way, I guess you could say that; you and Dad are my famous people."

"Now you are sounding like a star struck teenager. Are you going to want our autographs?"

Sue's first thought was, *Yes, I would like you and Dad to sign a marriage certificate.* Her mom left to hang up her coat; meanwhile, her dad arrived and was also surprised at the beautiful table setting and asked if someone famous was coming. Sue said yes and told him she hoped they would be the entertainment for the night. Her dad didn't have a clue and was questioning Sue just as her mom walked in the room.

"I remember the both of you had good voices, but even better when you sang together." Her parents looked at each other and at Sue and just shrugged their shoulders. Sue said, "We have about fifteen minutes until supper is ready, so why don't the two of you go in the den and practice a song." They went, but they took Dan with them. They wanted his opinion as to whether they still have it or were washed-up has-beens. *What is going on*, Sue thought. *Young couples try to get rid of chaperones, but older people—at least my parents—are always looking for one. Dinner just has to change all this.*

She brought out the candles and lit them right before calling them to come and eat. The meal received compliments. Sue told them that she had a special dessert and asked them to leave room for it. Just as they were finishing, Sue ushered Dan into the kitchen before her mother could insist on helping. "You two relax and wait here, and we'll be back shortly."

Sue milked the sundae preparation as long as she could. It didn't help that Dan was hungry for one and so was moving quickly. She kept trying to slow him down, but that was like slowing down a dog on a hunt. When the sundaes were finished, complete with cherries on top, they took them into the dining room. The sight she had been hoping for was not there. All she found was her mother reading a book, and she did not see her dad anywhere. "Where did Dad go?" she asked.

"Your dad went into the den to play with George and said to call him when ready."

Sue was so disappointed she didn't even want to give him a sundae. *How could he be so thoughtless as to go and play with a dog rather than be with Mom?* Inside, she was furious; but on the outside, she was very calm as she called out, "Dad, your dessert is ready." She scarcely noticed the taste of her sundae, because she absolutely could not believe what had just happened. While eating his sundae, her dad did ask her mom about the book she was reading, which led to a short conversation between the two of them. That ended up being the highlight of the evening. Saturday was equally uneventful, except that they made lots of headway on the nursery.

On the way to church Sunday morning, Sue was thinking about Friday night. *Now I know why my dad never remarried. What woman would like being with a man in a nice romantic setting if he just leaves to play with the dog? Yes, Lord, I know I still have to love and honor my father and mother, but he is such a . . . Now, I am not going to finish that sentence, but I could sure think of a bunch of ways to do so, and they wouldn't make for a lovely and a good report. Yes, Lord, I love my dad, but I sure hope your sermon this morning is on marriage, because he doesn't seem to have a clue.*

After praise and worship, Pastor John made the announcement that he had had a different sermon all set, but the night before, in prayer, God took him in a different direction. "It is called 'Mind Your Own Business and Seek God's,'" he said.

Sue thought *No!* But she didn't realize that the "no" also came out of her mouth loud and clear. She looked around to see some stares and felt a little jab from her husband. She sat up straight and decided she had better listen.

"If a person is thinking on what God says and what God wants them to do," the pastor said, "chances are they won't be off meddling. Jesus said he was about his Father's business, and as he is, so are we in this world. The best way to stay out of trouble is find out what God wants you to do and do it. When we try to direct our own lives, or someone else's, we are telling God we know better than him." Sue paid close attention through the rest of the sermon.

In the car on the ride home from church, Sue was very quiet. "Okay, Lord, I know I am the busybody Pastor John was referring to, but what am I supposed to do? I am just trying to shed a little light on something my parents seem to be in the dark about."

Sue was so deep in her thoughts that she didn't even notice her parents were having a conversation together. She did catch her mom saying, "Yes, that is a great idea." She turned and asked, "What are you two planning that is a great idea?"

"Nothing, dear, just discussing the nursery."

*Oh Pooh!* Sue thought. *They are treating me like a five-year-old, like everything is over my head, including my own baby's room.*

After everyone left, Sue asked Dan what her parents had been talking about in the car. "It was about the nursery," said Dan. "Why don't you just forget about it and let the sermon today direct you to look in the mirror?"

"Yes, I got the third degree from God, and now I am going to get it from you too."

"Repetition is a great teacher. Did you ever stop to think maybe God has his own plan?"

"The way things are going, I don't think anyone has a plan."

In a conversation with her mom the following morning, Sue wanted to find out if there were any new developments. Her mom thought she was talking about Dan's parents. Sarah was still calling her occasionally with Bible questions, and she thought they were getting really close to inviting Jesus into their lives. After saying good-bye, Sue told the Lord she was hanging up her Cupid arrows unless he gave her archery lessons. She breathed a big sigh of relief.

When Dan came home, Sue informed him she had packed away her unsuccessful matchmaking tools. He laughed and said, "I was unsuccessful in straightening you out, so I assume God has been talking to you?"

"Yes, he said four words to me: "I am the way.""

"We will see; it is one thing to hear from God, but another to obey."

"Thursday I am having lunch with your mom, and I hope she is more fun and trusting than you are."

The rest of the evening they both remained silent, not wanting to argue in front of their unborn baby.

Sue's lunch with her mother-in-law ended up being very interesting. The food was excellent at the new family owned restaurant they went to, and of course they talked about the time left before the new arrival. Then, out of the clear blue, Sarah asked, "Why are so many people against God? I look at my life, and I don't remember being taught against him, but I feel a part of me is always wondering, if God is good, then how come all these bad things keep happening? Where is that wonderful God your pastor preaches about? Does he really exist?"

"This is interesting, because I was just studying this yesterday. Do you know how often people form an opinion about someone based on what they are told? That is what all religions do, and then they pass how they view God on to the next generation. They look at God according to circumstances rather than his great love. To answer you about our pastor, who preaches with such zeal and excitement—that comes from an ongoing and fresh relationship with God. Does that make him perfect in everything he says? Absolutely not! Each person is responsible to develop their own relationship with the Lord and seek him for the truth. A preacher is supposed to speak the word of God, point people to Jesus, and let the Holy Spirit lead and guide into all truth."

On the way home, Sarah was very quiet. Sue was hoping this was because of some of the things she had said, and not because she was mad at her. Her mother-in-law dropped her off and said, "The lunch was good, but your sermon was definitely the main course, and I'm taking it home in a doggie bag. Good-bye, dear, and I will see you on Saturday. Love you."

"Love you too."

# Chapter Twenty-One

Dan and Sue were very excited, knowing they were coming down the home stretch in getting the nursery finished. Everyone showed up by 10:00, and the women left to go shopping while the men started transforming the nursery into a Green Bay Packers mecca. They did it in such a way that if a baby girl arrived, enough dainty little things could be added to transform it into a pretty Packer room. Either way, not being a Green Bay Packers fan would not be an option. After finishing; they dished out the lunch Sue had prepared for them and went to watch a baseball game.

When the women returned, they found the men sound asleep. Sue's mind went immediately to opportunity mode. Sue got out some washable green and gold paint and suggested they do some artwork on the men's faces and let them think they had used real paint. After they had gotten rid of the evidence, the watching and waiting began. Nothing happened for a while, so Sue decided to phone herself so it would ring and wake the guys up. It worked, and as Dan picked up the phone, he looked at the other two and saw they were looking back at him. They all pointed and started to laugh, but when they realized the joke was on all of them, they went silent.

Dan spoke first. "It looks like my prankster wife has struck again, only this time she went too far. What were you thinking? We can't use turpentine on our faces. How could you do such a dumb thing and laugh about it?"

Sue then showed them the washable paint that they had used. Then the guys said they knew it all along. "Right, you guys didn't know anything," said Sue. "We pulled a good one."

Dan said, "There is always payback, and it is looming just around the corner."

"You have to be nice; I am carrying your child."

"That might or might not work; stay tuned to find out," said Dan. A few minutes later, the guys came back with the paint still on and declared it wouldn't come off. Sue read the directions, and it listed a lot of washable surfaces, including skin. "Well, they were wrong about skin," said Dan. "You are stuck with us the way you made us."

The next morning, Dan put on his dark green suit to match his face and was ready. His wife looked at him, shook her head, and said, "What are you going to tell the people at church?" "Nothing, dear; I will refer them to you for an explanation. I just wish you would have done this during football season; then they would have just thought I was going to the game."

"What am I going to tell them?"

"I don't know; you should have thought about that before your practical joke."

"Okay, I am sorry; will you forgive me?"

"Yes, dear, I will."

They walked out to the car, and Dan said he had to run back into the house to get his Bible. He came back out and found Sue leaning back in the passenger seat with her eyes closed. She was thinking about trying to save face in front of all their friends at church. Oh, that was not funny. When they arrived and Dan turned off the engine, Sue opened her eyes and did a double-take. Dan's face was totally clean. Dan informed her that the paint was very much removable; he was just doing a little payback, which seemed to have worked. "Now I would say we are even, right?"

"You're right; I guess we will both have to straighten up so we are a good example to our child. I don't want him to get in trouble at school for playing pranks and then tell his teacher he learned it from his parents."

The cold days of winter were giving way to spring. Occasionally the temperature was pushing the upper sixties, which seemed oh, so very warm to Dan and Sue. Sue sat on her rocker by the window, looking at how everything outside had come to life. It reminded her of the wonderful little baby that was developing inside her.

Sue had to accept the fact that her parents were no longer interested in each other; if they would just be civil, that would have to be good enough. Sue turned her thoughts to something that *had* been developing: her in-laws had been attending church frequently, and they continued to ask questions. *A heart belief can take so much longer than a head belief,* Sue thought. *The head can believe when it sees, hears, tastes, smells, or touches.*

*But a heart belief has to deal with something that isn't generally influenced by the five physical senses. It is meeting Jesus in a way that registers deep inside a person.* Then she chuckled and thought, *being a Christian, there is always a sermon in my head.*

One Sunday, Dan and Sue had a big surprise in church. First, Pastor John gave a sermon titled "Circumstances Are Not an Indicator of God's Love."

"Sometimes life isn't so good because of what we listen to and the bad choices that catch up to us," the pastor said. "God's Word says he always provides a way of escape, but how often are people tuned into his channel? Satan deals through our five physical senses, which speak loud and may drown out what God is saying. What I need to add here is, do not get into condemning yourself! Don't think, 'What did I do to have this happen to me?' That is just as dangerous as thinking, 'Why did God do this to me?' Know that God loves you one hundred percent of the time, now and for all eternity. Learning to trust in God no matter what things look like is a life time process."

When the altar call was given, asking for anyone who wanted to receive Jesus to come forward and pray, Dan watched his parents walk down the aisle together. After they received some counseling and Christian books they came back, and Dan's father said, "Son, you just don't know how wonderful Jesus is until you meet him."

\* \* \*

The month of May brings opening day of fishing on the inland lakes. Dan tried to discourage his wife from sitting in a boat. They went back and forth with the pros and cons but couldn't come to an agreement. Dan, wanting to please his wife, came up with an idea that might please both of them. She wanted to know his plan right away and thought maybe he was just stalling, hoping she would forget about fishing. Dan wasn't sure his idea would work, but he knew it wouldn't take him long to check it out. He thought that Sue was too big to be comfortable sitting in a small boat.

Dan left, and Sue started going through books to find some fun games for the upcoming bridal showers. She found three games, and she also found something else that looked interesting. Each guest was given a special piece of paper with instructions to write a page about the bride and or groom. They could write memories, attributes, prayers, wishes for their future, or how they knew or were related to the bride and groom. They would be put in a scrapbook with pictures and presented at the wedding.

That evening, Dan came home a little late but in a jubilant mood. His lateness was due to his having gone to The Waterway Fishing Excursions Company. He told Sue that for sixty dollars apiece, they could go on a charter boat on Lake Michigan for four hours. Sue was thrilled and gave her husband a big hug. Dan said, "I just thought it was something we had never done; you would be comfortable, with plenty of room to walk around." The trip was the main topic before, during, and after supper. That would fill up the month of May: the first weekend the bridal shower, the second the fishing trip, the third a wedding, and the fourth the trip to Jake's.

The bridal shower was a big success with lots of gifts, and everyone seemed to enjoy the games. The second week was the fishing trip, which ended up fabulous with some nice trout fillets for the freezer. The wedding, which was the third week, turned out to be wonderful.

The following week couldn't go by fast enough. Jake wasn't giving any information in his letters, and Dan and Sue were hoping he had good news but just wanted to wait and tell them in person. Meanwhile, there was lots of excitement on the family front. Sue's mother-in-law was calling almost every day, sharing about her new and wonderful relationship with Jesus. He had talked to her a couple of times, and the Holy Spirit was showing her things in the Bible that were life changing. The last time they spoke, she said, "Wow! This is what I have been missing all my life. And to think this was just a heart's desire away. Talking about the Lord between two believers is always fun, and can sometimes take hours."

# Chapter Twenty-Two

On Saturday morning, Dan and Sue got on the road early to visit Jake. When they arrived, he had a nice lunch prepared for them. They wanted to hear all about his walk with Jesus and whether he had made any progress with his family. He asked them if they wanted the condensed version or if they wanted to hear it all.

"We came to spend the weekend with you," said Sue, "so we have time for the whole story."

"First off, before I even started the search, I told the Lord this was his command, his love, and his word. Everything that is him never fails. My parents are in an old folk's home just a couple of hours from here. I called to see if they would see me, and when the home returned my call, the answer was simply yes, which was good enough for me. When I arrived and walked into their room, the love of God washed over me, and all I could see was the two most wonderful parents in the world. I knew I was committed no matter what happened, but I had no idea God would make it so easy. Right then I realized love is so simple; it is the hurt, pain, anger, and resentment that complicate a person's life. As I walked toward them, I said, 'I love you, Mom; I love you, Dad.' There was no response, and then I hugged each one and said to them again, 'I love you,' and the most amazing thing happened. Each one responded with an "I love you too, son." That started a big flood of tears from all of us. I was not going to ask any questions, because love never cares about the past, it is all about now; but they brought it up and explained.

"They told me that when I was ten and they decided to split up, they were both so hurt and devastated that neither one could think beyond the pain. Their world crashed, and nothing mattered—and that nothing included me. They both wandered aimlessly in life for years, with bouts of depression, bitterness, and dolor. They led lives they were ashamed of.

"A few years ago, mom was grocery shopping and dad was passing through the town and stopped to get some snacks for the road to anywhere. They ended up in the same aisle and looked up at the same time. Both stared, and what came to their minds was the love they had once had for each other. Dad started up a casual conversation, and mom responded, so they went out to lunch together. They talked, but here is the kicker: neither one could remember what they had fought about; it was just that once it had all started, they both kept hurling hurtful words at each other until it became a contest to outdo what the other one said. The pain they piled on each other left no room for me, their marriage, their home, and their jobs—nothing. The house and contents was sold, and each left with a couple of suitcases.

"As I listened, I could see that Satan had used his influence to pound the very life out of both of them. Anyway, after the lunch went well, they agreed to see each other again. My dad found a job on the outskirts of town. It was a courtship, like they were finding each other for the first time.

"Then they inquired about my life and what had brought me to see them. I told them about life on the farm, my marriage and four children, and then my life as a recluse. Their eyes showed such sadness as my story unfolded, and my mom started to cry. But I said, 'Wait, things do get better; in fact, much better.' Then I told them about your unexpected visit and how you shared the love of God with me and I ended up inviting Jesus into my life. I didn't realize it at the time, but when I woke up the next day, everything was different—but I couldn't have explained it to anyone at the time. My mom said, 'that's all nice, son, but how did you end up here?'

"I continued by explaining going to church with you the next day, and how I didn't know what to expect and was very surprised when the pastor announced that God had told him to change his sermon to the fourth commandment—loving and honoring our mother and father with no exceptions whatsoever. I am sorry to admit this, but my first thought was 'That doesn't apply to me.' God let me know that every word the pastor spoke was meant for me and that if I wanted to operate outside of love, I would have to turn my back on him. When he said that, all I could think was, 'I've got to find my parents right away and tell them I love them.' Immediately, that love that I had committed to have was so real and so great that I had no room to think otherwise. They didn't comment or ask any more questions, and I left there letting them know I would be back very soon."

Dan and Sue realized why he couldn't put this in a letter, and they were glad, because they knew they wouldn't quite see the same emotion in a letter as they would in person. Then we asked if he had been able to contact any of his children yet. He said that he hadn't and was waiting for us to come up and pray with him first. After the three of us prayed, Jake went to make the calls. A short time later, he came back into the room with his head down, but we could still see the tears in his eyes. He told us what had happened. "I called the oldest first, and he started calling me names and saying how dare I call him, and then he hung up. I called the second one, and there were all kinds of questions as to where I have been and why didn't I love my children enough to raise them. When I started to speak, all I heard was a click. Now I don't know if I should even bother trying the other two. I caused them so much pain all their lives, and now am I just dishing out more? What do I do?"

Dan stood up and said, "First of all, you do not quit. You can't undo the past, but you can fight—and fight hard—to make a future. Just remember: everything we do for Satan is a defeat, but everything we do for God is a victory. Now go call your daughter."

Jake went into the other room, and this time when he came back he had his head held high and a smile on his face. He said, "I made the third call to my daughter, and she was surprised and angry at first, but when I declared my love for her, she softened enough to be willing to see me. I was feeling much better when I called my youngest. He was very responsive and understanding. He said the past is in the past and would very much like to see me."

In church the next day, Jake was able to give his testimony. He included his experience contacting his four children. When he finished, it was the same as when he had spoken in Dan and Sue's church; there was not a dry eye to be found. But on the way home they laughed when Jake said, "It is a good thing God hasn't called me to preach; all I would do is make people cry."

Sue fixed lunch before she and Dan had to leave. After eating, they said a tearful good-bye to Jake and drove off. It had been quite an emotional weekend, and on the way home Sue just leaned her head back and thought about being a parent. *Everything you say and do is an influence for God or against God. This makes parenting an awesome responsibility. If you give them some religious beliefs, but want them to fit into this world, that is against God. But if you train them to seek and listen to God, they will get persecuted, and who wants that for their child?*

# Chapter Twenty-Three

Dan and Sue spent the following week having exciting thoughts of Jake seeing two of his children. Saturday evening came, and after supper, Dan and Sue literally stared at the phone like they were watching for it to ring. Finally, around 11:00, they gave up and went to bed. In the morning, the phone did ring, but they both thought they were dreaming, and neither one answered it. So Jake hung up and decided to just meet Dan and Sue at church.

After the service and back at the house, Sue prepared soup and sandwiches so there wouldn't be much chewing involved and they could finish quickly. Jake dramatically unfolded the events of the previous morning. "While I was getting ready to leave, I got down on myself and said nice and loud, 'I don't deserve to have any of my children in my life.' Then I was bombarded with every negative thought, including some of the same ones that had propelled me to leave my family many years ago. Then I yelled, 'God didn't bring me this far that I should quit.'

"When I got to my daughter's house and walked up to the door, I sure found out what 'knees-a-knocking' meant. I could have recorded a record and called it 'The Knee-Knockin' Polka.' When the door opened, I was welcomed by three children yelling 'Grandpa!' and giving me hugs. Then one asked me, 'Why are you crying, Grandpa; don't you like our hugs?' I told them they were happy tears because they gave such wonderful hugs. They all smiled, and I stood up to face my daughter for the first time in many years. We took a step forward, gave a tiny welcome grin, and hugged each other. I told her I loved her and would face any questions or criticism she wanted to throw my way. I deserved to be put on trial, and all I could do was plead for mercy.

"She said she had of course missed me being in her life many times, especially when she really needed me. She survived and has a wonderful family, and by my coming, I made it complete. I couldn't believe my ears.

It sounded like she was just going to let me come into her and her family's life. I told her I had no excuses but did have explanations if and when she would like to hear them. The children were busy playing, and she said she had time, so I gave her my slimmed-down version. When I got to the part about your visit because of a couple of bears, she was still intent. But I could see her squirm when I told her about the two of you leading me to Jesus. I finished with, 'Now that God's love is in me, I feel I have something to offer. I no longer am a recluse hiding from everyone, even myself.' Through the tears I was shedding, I was able to see she was crying too. Then she surprised me and came over and gave me a big hug.

"I told her I wanted to hear about whatever part of her life she wanted to share. As she started to talk, I knew it was not going to be good, because her mother and I were alike. The difference between us is that her mother was the recluse that stayed and raised them. I am not going to go into all the details, but my daughter had a very rough life. I couldn't even be sure that she would have been any better off if I had stayed. Of course it would have been somewhat different, but probably equally as painful. When she finished, there were more tears, and this time I went over to hug her. She called me daddy and was so happy to see me. Then there was a warning that I might have trouble winning over her husband, who was out of town for the weekend. 'He's a good guy, but very protective of us,' she said. 'I think when I tell him how well our meeting went, he will soften.'

"Before I left, I told her about my place by the lake and how much I would love to have them come and visit. She was excited and called the children to come listen to their grandpa. They sat next to me, and I told them the story about the boy and the songs he would play for the fish on his saxophone. I also told them that when they came to visit, Grandpa would build a big bonfire and they could roast marshmallows. They wanted to come right away, but their mom told them they would have to wait for a nice weekend. While we were saying our good-byes, she said she would work on her two older brothers. 'It's just that they remember more,' she said, 'and had more time to build up hurt and anger.' Then she said something that touched me and made me proud. She has come to the conclusion that forgiveness is part of survival, and she is happy she took that road.

"Driving over to meet my youngest son, I was very thankful and very hopeful. I was invited in and met his wife and my baby grandson. They asked me to sit down, and we all agreed it was awkward. I wanted to say something to break the ice, but words were not coming, so I said a quick silent prayer: 'Help!' I told them how well the visit with his sister had gone and that I was delighted to meet my three grandchildren. I could just see the tightness in his face begin to soften. His wife seemed to relax, as to say she was just going to follow her husband. From there I just took the same direction I had taken with my daughter. 'I stand with no excuses for what I did,' I said, 'but I do have explanations for some of my many wrong decisions.' They listened intently, as if examining every word. I was thinking it might have been easier if I had four daughters.

"When I finished, my son had a blank look on his face that gave me no clue as to how things was going. I had pleaded for mercy, the same as I had done with my daughter. Finally I just asked if there was anything else he wanted to know and if he had things he was willing to share with me. The silence was the thick kind that you could cut with a knife. If he was doing this to make me squirm, it was working. If he was doing this because he really didn't know how he felt, I sure could understand that to. When he spoke, he explained: 'There was a battle going on in my mind. To survive, I learned to close everything out and lived as if a father never existed. Now to open that up and tell myself, "Yes, I do have a dad," is very risky. I am struggling with whether I want to take that chance. Are you going to come into my life and then disappear again? If I take this wall down and let you in, am I going to regret it? Can we get along and build something worthwhile?'

"I didn't hesitate to answer. 'Son, I came here with only one motive, and that is to give you a father's love, beginning today, for as long as I live. I can't redo the years I should have been here for you and wasn't, which I deeply regret. My love is so big for you that if you will just give it a chance, I will do anything and everything to make it work. Anytime you want to come down on me, I promise to take it like a man—I mean, like a father.' When I said the word 'father,' tears welled up in my eyes and could not be held back. I had said all I knew to say, and so I waited. When I looked up, I could barely make out my son, but it sure did look like he was crying too. I stood up and said, 'I will take ten steps if you will just take one.' He stood up and took one step, and I took the rest and gave him a big hug. 'Son, I love you,' I said. 'Dad,' he said, 'I think I love you too.' Then I hugged my daughter-in-law and asked if I could hold my grandson. The baby looked up at me with what looked like a smile, as if he was giving his approval too.

"After we had all dried our tears, they invited me to stay for supper, which I wouldn't have passed up in a million years. Once we warmed up, the conversation flowed very smoothly, and I got to hear about some good things in his life. He said he had found himself becoming somewhat of a recluse too. In high school he was a loner and never even asked a girl for a date.

"Shortly after graduation, he got a job near his home so he could walk there. The shortest way was through the park. One day he had some peanuts left from his lunch and noticed some squirrels scrambling around looking for food. So he sat down on the park bench and threw a few their way. This started a routine. "One day he got to the park bench, and a woman was not only sitting on his bench, but she was feeding his squirrels.

"She was very friendly and said, 'Hi, my name is Tammy, and you must be my fellow squirrel feeder.'

"'Yes I am,' he said. My name is Sam, and what are you doing feeding my squirrels?'

"He was serious, but she thought it was funny and started laughing. Just then they both looked, and the squirrels were lined up waiting, as if to say 'Quit the small talk and just give us our supper.' Sam and Tammy looked at each other and laughed. They quickly opened their bags of peanuts to concentrate on the task at hand. Sam said to me, 'We get unusual looks when we tell people our relationship started out kind of squirrelly.'

"After many meetings in the park, Sam knew she was stealing his heart, and he had to find out if there was any hope. He took a big step and asked her if she would like to ride out to Fishers Lake with him that coming Saturday. When she answered, 'I'd love to!' Sam felt some excitement because he knew she had to be interested too. Then he thought maybe she was just interested in feeding the squirrels by the lake.

"When Saturday arrived, Sam started to get cold feet and was going to pick up the phone to call Tammy and cancel. But he told himself, 'This is just friends going to feed little animals together.' His mom packed a lunch for them. On the way over, he decided he didn't like the sounds of 'My mother prepared a lunch for us.' It made them sound like a couple of little kids. He wanted to take her to a nice restaurant and try to impress her.

"Before he had figured out what to say about the food, he was in front of her house. She came out right away caring a big bag of peanuts.

Conversation flowed between them as they learned more and more about each other. They had similar values and interests. After walking around the lake and feeding every squirrel within miles, they stopped by a play area. He pushed her on the swing and then asked if she was getting hungry. She said yes. He told her his mom had packed them a lunch but that if she preferred, they could go to a nice restaurant. He was so relieved when she told him she thought that was so sweet of his mother. He found a picnic table, and they had their first meal together.

"When they had been dating about a year, Sam decided he wanted to ask Tammy to marry him. It had to be something so special she couldn't say no. He said, 'I know this is corny, but I did the only thing I could think of.' He took her back to the park bench where they had first met and had her sit down and close her eyes. All around, it looked like the squirrels were giving them their privacy. He brought out a hidden bag of peanuts and got down on the ground and with them formed the words 'Will you marry me?' Then he told her to open her eyes and look down. She read it and burst out laughing.

"He thought that he was really dumb and that he had just blown their whole relationship. He was so busy coming down on himself and being embarrassed, he didn't notice her crying and bending down. She took some peanuts and spelled out 'Yes.' She took his hand and pointed to her answer. He leaped over the bench and walked around to see if he was reading right. Then they hugged, and he remembered he had forgotten something. He told her to look closer at the peanuts, and when she did, she spotted her engagement ring around one of the peanut shells. His plan was that if she said no, he would laugh like it was just a joke, gather up the peanuts along with the ring, and put them back in the bag.

"When they announced their engagement, they told people that it was squirrelly. While planning their wedding, Tammy said, 'We must include the squirrels.' The decision was made to get married in the park and have people bring shelled peanuts to throw instead of rice. That would be their wedding present to the little creatures that brought them together.

"I told my son that was a great story and he should send it to a magazine. Then I asked him to tell me about his wedding. He said he was done talking for now and wanted me to share. So I showed him pictures of my place and invited him and his family to come anytime. I continued by sharing the visit that changed my life. You introduced me to a real and living God. His love for me gave me an overflow of love for my children.

That was what brought me here and gave me the strength to face and accept whatever you wanted to say or do to me. My one and only motive is love. After I finished explaining about that, my son took all the steps to come over and hug me. I shared some more, and then Tammy called us for supper. Not in my wildest dreams did I ever think I would be sitting there sharing a meal with my family. I asked if they minded if I said a pray of thanksgiving. They nodded to indicate it was okay, and I prayed a heartfelt prayer that I hoped pleased God and touched my son and his wife

Dan and Sue felt they were at a movie theater watching a person's life change and unfold right in front of their eyes. Sue said, "Wouldn't it be wonderful if TV and movies were about all the wonderful things God has done in people's lives? Take your story; it would make a wonderful book, followed by a great movie." Before Jake left, he promised to fill us in on the next chapter as soon as it developed.

The following morning, after Dan left for work, Sue decided to just take it easy after a great weekend. She went into the nursery and sat on the rocking chair and talked to her baby. "Listen, your dad and I are working very hard on expanding your family. Even though Jake isn't a relative, he has a large family he will share with us. I wonder if there is any hope for Jake and his former wife. Is she remarried? How do I find that out? I don't think Jake even knows. I will just have to wait and see."

Of course, with all this family talk, her mind wandered back to her parents, who seemed to have lost everything they had once had for each other. *I know I quit, but I am not giving up! I will invite them over for brunch after church Sunday. I will call my mom right away.* She went to the phone and dialed.

"Hello?"

"Mom," said Sue, "How would you like to come for brunch after church Sunday?" "I would love that, dear; is anyone else going to be there?"

"Well, dad should be able to come."

"Oh dear, I just forgot I won't be able to make it, sorry." Sue was about to ask her why, but she hung up.

# Chapter Twenty-Four

Dan and Sue hadn't heard from Jake all week, so they were quite surprised when he arrived at church Sunday morning. After the service, he said that he had more news and wanted to take them out for Sunday brunch. They both said yes and anticipated good news. It turned out to be some good and some not so good. "My daughter told me that my oldest son, Mark, was softening, but John hasn't yet. Anyway, Mark ended up calling me yesterday, and we met at a park halfway between our houses. I was shocked at how much he looked like me, and I think he was too. It broke the ice, because we both laughed that it was like looking in a mirror. He apologized he hadn't been willing to see me when I called; he had just wanted to protect himself and his family. He told me that when he talked to his brother Sam, who was impressed with my warmth and genuine interest, he became willing to take a chance. At that moment we hugged each other, and I gave him the same explanation I had given his siblings. Then I asked how he was doing. He said he was married to his childhood sweetheart, Willow, and that they had two sons, Tim and Alex.

"I sat and listened to the story about him and his wife, Willow. It all started because of her name. She had told him that her dad wanted a boy so badly that he wouldn't even consider girl names. So the morning her mom went into labor and they were pulling out of the driveway to go to the hospital, her mom yelled, 'That's it! Our baby's name has been sitting right in front of us all these months. Look at the tree across the street.' Her father told her he wasn't naming any child Tree. 'No! No!' she said, 'It's a willow! They are so dynamic, and yet very gentle. That will be her name if it's a girl.' After all that drama, her dad agreed. As she grew up, the neighbors hung a couple of swings on the tree and called it Willow's willow, and she was allowed to swing on it anytime she wanted.

"When my son first met her, he laughed at her name. She took him over to the swings, and they enjoyed themselves so much that he never made fun of her again. Through the years they had some fights but always made their way back to the swings. In high school they both dated other people, and then a couple of weeks before graduation it dawned on my son that he didn't want to be with anyone else. He called her to meet him at her tree. She sat on the swing, and he got down on his knee and asked her to marry him. They hadn't been dating, so it took her by such surprise that she started laughing and asked which willow he was talking to. When a guy gets serious, the last thing he wants is to be laughed at, so he started to put the ring back in his pocket. She said, 'Not so fast. You asked me a question. I am saying yes, and now I want my ring!' He put the ring on her finger and breathed a sigh of relief. He told me she makes life interesting because she still likes to keep him guessing.

"I told him that was a great story and that I would also like to hear about my grandchildren. He told me about Tim, who is two, and Alex, who is four. He was glad they didn't have a girl. They would have had to find a tree to name her after, and they couldn't think of any they liked. Could you imagine a little girl being named Evergreen, Blue Spruce, or Oak? I guess Georgia Pine would be nice if she never told anyone her middle name. Anyhow, he started laughing and said, 'Dad, do you see the humor here? We get together after all these years and talk about trees.' I told him that it was such a wonderful story and that I was so looking forward to meeting her and my grandchildren.

"What he said next was music to my ears. 'I have an idea, Dad. If you can come to our house next Saturday, I will see if I can't get everyone together, including John. Then you can see all your children and grandchildren at one time. We don't always get along, but we seem to find a way to forgive, and we work on the forgetting part. We can grill out, and there is plenty of room outside.' I told him that would be wonderful and that if John decided to come but wanted to talk to me first, I would be very willing. I would be thankful for any time I got to spend with my family."

Sue asked if any of them talked about their mother.

"Not since the time she made the lunch for Sam and Tammy. So I don't know how she is doing or if she even knows I am in the picture."

Sue asked, "How do you feel about seeing her? Am I out of line to ask that? You know I wanted my parents to get back together. But over and over again, they made it clear they are only tolerating each other for my sake. I am sorry to say my cupid wings might want to focus on you and your wife."

"I think you should keep those cupid wings in retirement. The fact that we were both introverted put barriers up right from the beginning. Even though we had four children together, we never connected emotionally. That trust and closeness never developed. I felt that if I left, maybe she could find someone that would appreciate her and love her. I hope that has happened, and I wouldn't mind sharing my children with a stepdad. I will just have to wait and see. I will let you know when I find out."

The week seemed to just fly by, and Sue was getting big enough to get a tad uncomfortable. Every day when she would go out to get the mail, she would walk around the block first. She thought about the two groups of people that continued to advise her. One group would say, "Get plenty of exercise for an easier delivery," and the other group kept saying, "Get as much rest as you can, you won't get any once the baby arrives." Her walks were starting to get shorter and slower.

When she returned to the house, she looked through the mail. Sue wondered how she got on so many mailing lists for baby items. There was one that looked like a card with no return address. She thought maybe it was an invitation from the third couple from church getting married this summer. It was their wedding invitation, all right, but the printer had made some very big mistakes. It was just the form, with their names missing. The little card did include the date, place, and time, but no space to respond. The wedding was a week from Saturday, which Sue found strange, as invitations usually go out at least a month ahead of the big day. There was no sense in saying anything, because it was too late to change it, and she sure wouldn't want to point this out and embarrass them right before their special day. *I sure hope it isn't because she is pregnant and this is a rush wedding*, Sue thought. When Dan came home, Sue gave him the invitation to read, along with her thoughts on it. He agreed to just keep quiet, bring a gift, and be supportive, because, as he told Sue, he was glad they were at least doing the right thing.

Getting up early and making Dan breakfast was becoming quite the chore for Sue. Sometimes she would tell Dan the baby wasn't ready to get up yet. He would just tell her she might as well go back to sleep, and he would make his own breakfast. When she finally got up and ate on one such morning, she realized she was too big to wear the same dress she had worn to the last wedding. She called her mom and asked her to go with her to buy a new dress and purchase a gift for a wedding a week from Saturday. Her mom asked her how come she had waited so long. She started to explain but then decided to wait until the following day and explain over lunch.

At 8:55 the following morning, Sue's mom picked her up. The reason for the early departure was that stores would be less crowded in the morning. By the time they were on the third store, Sue suggested she just wear a potato sack and paint flowers on it. Her mom was persistent and found two dresses for Sue to try on. They both agreed on one that was perfect for Sue's roly-poly figure.

Over lunch Sue told her mom about the invitation she had gotten just a week and a half before the wedding. "Oh, I sure hope you're wrong about the possibility of a pregnancy," her mom said. "Have I met this couple?"

"No, I don't think so. They are quite a bit younger than us. Phil is a really nice young man that Dan has worked with on some maintenance and lawn projects. I have worked with Julie in the nursery. We both get lots of practice changing diapers. All I know is that the two of them were neighbors in grade school, and then Phil's family moved away. They were both surprised that this many years later they ended up joining the same church."

"You will have to let me know how the wedding is; hopefully there will be a better explanation than what you are thinking."

They finished eating, paid the check, and decided to go shop for a really nice present. Sue was thinking one of those toasters that toast four slices at a time, just in case they were starting a family. But her mom didn't agree. "You don't want to buy anything that might embarrass them." She suggested a nice picture or wall hanging that would make them think of Sue and Dan whenever they looked at it.

"That's a great idea, Mom; why didn't I think of that?"

"Well, I guess that's what moms are for."

The search was on, and it took looking at hundreds before they found one that they both loved immediately. It was a peaceful lake scene with a log cabin that had a nice porch with a couple of rocking chairs on it. Sue asked her mom if she thought it might be too old-fashioned. "No, dear," she said. "Even young couples have their dreams about a nice, peaceful vacation place like this."

"You're right, Mom, and usually young couples have lots of wall space to fill. Almost everyone gets toasters and Crock-Pots, but this is something different. It is from the heart. I didn't realize what a smart, sensitive mother I have. I hope I grow up to be just like you."

"You are grown up and you are doing fine. Go pay for this so I can take you home and you can rest while I prepare supper before I leave."

"You are spoiling me, Mom."

"No, I am showing you love. Spoiling makes someone undisciplined and promotes only caring about themselves."

Upon arriving back home, Sues mom covered Sue up in the recliner to rest while she went into the kitchen and prepared a nice casserole. The next thing Sue knew, Dan was waking her up to come and eat. She said, "You mean I can go in my kitchen now?" Dan didn't know what she was talking about, so she explained. "After shopping, my mom thought I should rest and said she would make us supper, and then she must have left. Before we eat, I have to show you what I bought."

Dan just nodded his approval and said, "Let's eat."

While they were eating, Sue thought she should do this anytime she bought something. When she showed Dan her purchases right before a meal, he didn't ask questions like "What for?" and "How much?"

Late Saturday evening, the phone rang and Sue answered it. "Hi Jake."

"How did you know it was me?"

"Well, George and I—I mean, I—was praying for you and just knew. Now tell me what happened."

"The bad news is that my son John did not show up, but everything else is good news. When you haven't had family and then you get some, it is like every second is a treasure. That is how I felt with my children and grandchildren. My children promised to be on their best behavior for me, but I noticed some sibling rivalry going on. I just had to laugh about it, and they joined me. I requested to pray before we ate, and they nodded their okay.

"They shared lots of stories. Most were humorous, and a few were sad—like when my daughter's dog died and when my youngest son's bike broke and there was no one to fix it. I felt a lump in my throat, but I knew he had every right to say those things. With God, I don't have to bury myself in all the things I didn't do, but I can live in what I can do today.

"One of my grandsons came and took me by the hand, and we walked outside into the garage and he showed me his broken bike. I asked, 'Do you want grandpa to fix it?' He said yes with a big smile on his face and showed me where his dad's toolbox was. I got it fixed just in time for my son to come out and see his son so happy to be riding his bike again. He gave me a big hug and said, 'Thanks, Dad.' I felt like the Lord gave me a little chance to redeem myself, and it put a look of love on my son's face.

"Around eight p.m. I felt the Holy Spirit nudging me to tell me it was time to go. We had great good-byes, and they promised to keep working on John. The plan is for them to come by my place next month, and they will try to convince their brother to come with them."

"I will give the news to Dan tonight when he comes home," said Sue. "There is a wedding at out church this weekend, so if you would like, Dan and I could come the following Saturday. My traveling days are coming to an end until after my baby is born. The moms are already monitoring everything I do and watching over me like a hen waiting for her chicks to be born."

Sue filled Dan in on Jake's news during supper. At first he didn't like the idea of going up there in two weeks, but she convinced him he could take care of her there just as well as at home. On Saturday morning, while getting ready, Sue suggested that now that they were Christians, they should plan a wedding. Dan said, "Not while you are pregnant; I don't want people to think this is a shotgun wedding."

"No, I was thinking after our son is old enough to be the ring bearer."

"That all sounds good, but for now let's concentrate on getting to this one on time."

"You're right; I am almost ready."

We arrived at church with not much time to spare. It seemed to Sue that Dan was driving awfully slowly. *He's not even a dad yet,* she thought, *so he shouldn't be doing grandma/grandpa type driving.* They weren't related to the couple and didn't even know them outside of church, so Sue had assumed they would sit in the back. But Dan just marched them right up to the front. Sue gave him looks and even nudges, but he seemed to be ignoring her. She couldn't do anything but sit, because the procession music started.

Sue turned to see the bridesmaids, who she felt were always such a beautiful part of a wedding. Sue then saw her mother-in-law and father-in-law. At first she thought, *what are they doing here? They better hurry up and sit down, because they are holding up the wedding.* They didn't sit down, though; they went and stood at the altar. Sue thought that maybe they had heard rumors and had come to stop the wedding. She was sure wishing she had just stayed home. When she turned to look for the bride, she spotted Jake. *He never told us he was invited. I am almost positive he does not know this couple.*

It seemed to Sue that they were stalling a long while, because the music repeated itself a few times. It made her wonder if the bride or groom had gotten cold feet and left. Just then the music got louder, and everyone stood up, waiting for the bride. Sue was wondering where the groom was. From a distance all brides looked beautiful to Sue, but this one's veil looked so lacy that it was hard to see her face. When she got closer, she turned to Sue and smiled. *She sure looks a lot like my mom, only much younger*, thought Sue.

When the bride got to the altar, Sue turned and saw her dad standing there. *What kind of joke is this, and where is the young couple that is getting married? Is my dad really marrying this young woman just because she looks like mom? Then why wouldn't he just marry mom? What if that is my mom? They would not play such a mean trick on me and pretend to marry each other.* Sue was getting angrier and more confused by the minute. *No, these are just phony smiles just to torture me, but why? I have been behaving myself and not interfering.* Just then, Pastor John started talking about the seriousness of marriage. The vows were beautiful, and the voices sounded to Sue like her parents'. *This is a horrible joke and downright mean. I don't know if I can ever forgive them.* She looked up, and the groom lifted the veil and kissed the bride, and they smiled at each other. *This is just like a real wedding; no, this* is *a real wedding, and those are faces filled with love.* Sue started to cry, and through the tears, she saw them coming toward her. The groom said, "Sue, I would like you to meet my wife, who happens to be your mom."

"Sue," said the bride, "I would like you to meet my husband, who just happens to be your dad."

At first Sue wanted to be angry, because they had done everything to show her they didn't want a relationship while they had been developing one behind her back. When she reminded herself that was exactly what she had prayed for, she wanted to run up and down the aisle like Paul Revere, only yelling "My parents are married! My parents are married!"

There was still a little part of her that was angry and upset, but the Lord reminded her he had given her exactly what she wanted. She said to him, "You're right, Lord; I am just a bratty kid, and I repent. But if it is okay with you, I am going to just do a little bit of payback."

Her parents were in the vestibule, getting lots of congratulations. Sue walked past them and just said, "Well!" and walked out the door. She then went around to the back door and caught them just as they were going to leave. She grabbed them and gave them great big hugs. They were surprised, as they thought she had left upset. "No!" she said. "I was thankful and excited, but I just wanted to do a little payback for not telling me."

"Why would we tell you?" said her dad. "We were having so much fun watching you go to such great lengths to accomplish what was already done."

"What do you mean already done?"

"The moment your mom and I first laid eyes on each other, we knew our love had never died. The only problem was we didn't know how the other one felt. So one day we met for lunch and started laughing about the great lengths you were going to bring us back together. After the laughter, we both looked very seriously at each other. I told your mom that nothing had changed for me, that I would always love her—and that my love is stronger than ever, now that I have Jesus. Then she told me she felt the same."

"None of this makes any sense. You knew I wanted you together, so why did you always act like you were just being civil for my sake?"

"First of all, we are parents, and you never want to encourage your children that nosiness and manipulation is a good thing under any circumstances."

"So you were trying to discipline me as though I was a little kid?"

"Well, you were acting like one. Besides, we did get some enjoyment out of guessing what you were going to do next and what we should do. Now, are you going to enjoy the day with us before we leave on our honeymoon or not?"

"Of course I am. I just have a question—actually two questions. Did you keep this secret from everyone, or just me?"

"Well, we didn't put it in the newspaper, so there were some that didn't know. Now what was your other question?"

"Will you tell me where you are going on your honeymoon?"

"We're sorry, dear, that is classified information that we made sure not to tell your husband, so don't bother giving him the third degree."

"You mean you still don't trust me?"

"Nope!"

Sue's mom said, "We have until five before the reception, and we have some places we would like to take you and Dan."

"If it is more good news, I am ready, and if I am dreaming all this, don't wake me up until after the dinner, which I presume will be prepared by my favorite caterers."

"Let's put it this way: we hope you will like it. To some children it could be a nightmare."

"Now you really have my curiosity and attention; let's go."

Sue's dad drove in the direction of Sue and Dan's house, which didn't make any sense. Sue thought, *they wouldn't try to move in with us without even asking; that could be a problem.* Just then they pulled into a driveway and started getting out of the car. As she followed them up the driveway, Sue asked if they knew the people who lived there. They both said yes as her dad got out a key and opened the front door. Sue was stumped but followed them. Her mom asked, "Would you like to welcome us to your neighborhood?"

"What! This is your house?"

"Yes it is. Your dad got a job transfer, and we wanted to be close to our grandchild. We especially liked the big backyard, and we are going to fence it in."

"That is a lot of yard for one child; I hope you aren't expecting more."

"We understand that is none of our business, but we want to be ready. And besides that, we want to get a puppy. Your dad and I would like to take you out to lunch to celebrate."

"I will go, but I will only feed the baby; I am too excited to eat."

"Okay, we want to see how you do that."

The whole afternoon was great, and the meal at the reception was wonderful, including a wonderful fruit-filled punch. Sue's parents made the announcement that there would not be any usual entertainment, but instead a time to give glory and honor to God. Without him, the wedding would not have happened. The bride and groom told how they had each recently met Jesus and how he had brought them back together. Sue heard more details than they had given her earlier. They talked about how much fun they had had keeping everything from her while she tried so hard to get them to reconnect. They laughed when they explained about the little winks behind her back whenever they were at her house. They would leave

Sue's house scowling at each other and then meet a block away and go on a date.

The best part was with three weddings coming up, allowed them to plan their without Sue knowing it. The kicker was the blank invitation sent at just the right time, and Dan worked with them to get Sue to the wedding. "Our inspiration for all of this was found in the Bible," said Sue's dad. "We realized God has a big sense of humor, and the one reference we used was Jonah. He was messing up, and God sent him on an all-expenses-paid vacation to a place of solitude to think things over and come to his senses and be obedient. We put our daughter in an uncomfortable situation by never cooperating with her ideas and schemes, hoping she would come to her senses and trust in the Lord."

It turned out to be a wonderful wedding and a perfect reception. The whole evening was filled with testimonies of the love and greatness of God, including Dan's and Sue's and Jake's. And there were other testimonies given that Dan and Sue hadn't heard before.

One young woman had grown up angry and hateful. Her parents were drug addicts and, most of the time, didn't even know she was around. Living in anger and fear didn't make for very good adolescent or teen years. "I will not go into details of what I did, but I am ashamed of it now. Anyway, in my senior year of high school, I was running with the wild crowd, but I kept noticing this square. Not only was he square, but he was a religious nut. Unfortunately, he was very good looking, and every time he looked at me, I melted just a little bit more.

"He knew I ran with the wrong crowd, so I didn't know why he was trying to be nice to me? One day I just flat-out asked him. His answer was that he just wanted to look at and pray for his bride-to-be. My mouth dropped open, and I was just about ready to start cursing him when he added that the Lord had told him to keep praying for her to receive Jesus and she would be his wife someday. Right before he walked away, he added that he hoped I would give in soon. I wanted to run after that square and give him a piece of my mind. Some neighbors had taken me to church a few years before, and I heard about God and Jesus, and I believed. What made him think he was a Christian and I was not?

"I didn't run into him for a few days. He wasn't in the usual places at the usual times. So then I started to miss his smile and kind face. Then one day I saw him at a custard stand. I went up to him and—in a nice, loud voice—said, "Where have you been? If you expect me to be your wife, you can't play any disappearing acts." Then I realized what I had said and how loud I had said it. I ran out of there as fast as my feet would take me and didn't stop until I got home and was safely in my bedroom. I lay on my bed and cried for what seemed like a long time. Out of anger, I went and dug my Bible out of my closet, thinking I was going to tell him a thing or two and then he would leave me alone.

"The few times I had tried to read the Bible, it didn't make sense and didn't appear to have anything to do with life today. But now it was absolutely exciting, and so much was starting to make sense. 'What is so different?' I wondered. 'Is Harry really praying for me? Wow, his name is even plain. What a match we would make. I was born to be wild and he was born to be blah. What could we ever have in common?' I began to see God's love in the words, and they seemed to be directed right at me. I didn't know it at the time, but God was churning me like butter. I was becoming the last thing in the world I wanted to be: caring and sensitive. Of course, I didn't realize any of this at the time, but God's word was working me over. I finally closed the Bible and said, 'That is enough of that. No one is going to run my life. No God, no religion, and certainly not Harry the wimp.' I closed my eyes and just got madder and madder. When I opened them, I said to God, 'I am going to open this Bible one last time, and if you've got something to say to me, say it now.' I opened it, and the page was Deuteronomy 4: 29: 'But IF from thence thou shalt seek, the Lord thy God, thou shalt find him, IF thou seek him with all thy heart, and with all thy soul.' So God comes with ifs. My thinking was that he loves everybody and we are all God's children. I think I better keep reading.

"There were way too many ifs, and they all seemed to lead to more questions. I didn't find all the answers I was looking for, but I found out enough to realize I was in big trouble. Even if I was nice and went to church, that wouldn't cut it with God. If I prayed and gave money to the poor, that wouldn't do it. I reread Deuteronomy 4:29 again. I just wished those ifs weren't in there. I kept reading "seek him with all my heart" over and over again, and it was really penetrating. I fell to my knees and said to God, 'I give you my heart; can I be your valentine?' This may sound stupid, but it wasn't. It felt like a gentle bolt of lightning went through me and burned out some old and brought in some new.

"I started talking to God like he was really there, and he was. I discovered I also had a love for Harry. The next day, I took off running to tell him, but he was nowhere to be found. In my excitement and desperation, I asked anyone and everyone if they had seen him. I had to laugh about the strange looks. I was thinking, 'Wait until they find out I am now one of those religious freaks.' Anyway, I am trying to shorten this because I know there are more testimonies. When I finally found Harry, he knew immediately I was different, and he proposed right away. I said to him, "Yes, I will, but let's not get married today. We need to get to know each other and graduate first." That Sunday, he brought me to this church, where I learned how wonderful God is and how great it is to worship him. This is also where we got married. Everything was going fine until Pastor John preached on the fourth commandment. It hit me really hard. I didn't know that if I held onto someone else's sins, God couldn't forgive mine. After putting up a good fight, with lots of legitimate reasons, I gave in and told God nothing was more important to me than obeying him. He reminded me that as his child, I am required to love. After I forgave my parents, I went to find their whereabouts. They were surprised to see me, and there was no past to bring up, because I had put that in the sea of forgetfulness, which is the same place God put my past. They are receiving the love of God in me and hopefully will receive Jesus into their lives soon. I am sorry this took so long, but it is hard to find parts to leave out."

There were more wonderful testimonies that filled the entire evening.

In all the excitement of the day, Sue forgot that her parents had refused to tell her where they were going on their honeymoon. She figured Dan would have to know because they would have left a phone number with him in case the baby came early. On the ride home, she nicely asked, "Where did my parents go on their honeymoon?"

"Your parents were a little concerned that you would look for payback, but I think it is safe to tell you. You are too far along to be taking any long trips by yourself."

"You're right, dear, I couldn't even think about revenge unless they were close, and I still would probably need your help."

"I am sorry, dear, but as long as those wheels are turning in your head, I can't give you any information."

"I thought trust was the foundation of any relationship."

"Yes, dear, and I trust you explicitly; it's your parents that have some issues."

"Well! I don't need your help; I have my own ways of finding out things."

"Suit yourself. Look out, world; the female Sherlock Holmes is on the loose."

On Monday morning Sue sat down and thought about Saturday being so glorious and yet so frustrating. It was simply wonderful from beginning to end, except for her parents' secrecy. *I wouldn't have given it another thought if they had just told me where they were going. If I have to work, then they are going to have to pay.* "Is this okay, God?" she asked. "I know you have a sense of humor, so can I ask for your help? Can we put my parents in a whale's belly? Just long enough to cover them with seaweed so I can get a picture when the whale coughs them up. No, huh? Could you just tell me if they are on or near water? Okay, God, if they were far away on a beach, they would have told me, because I am sure not going to travel too far. That's a clue. Their concern about me finding out means they must be in the area. Now I have to make some phone calls and see if anyone that knows will let it slip."

Sue called her mother-in-law and innocently talked about the wonderful wedding. To bait her, she said, "Wasn't that a wonderful place for a honeymoon?"

"Yes, nice," she said. "They could be near water and still stay close by." Then she said she had something on the stove and had to go. *Wow!* Sue thought. *I must be onto something for her to hang up.*

The only other person Sue could think of to drill was Jake. She called him and asked if he knew anything. He was tighter than a clam. Before she hung up, she told him that if she were getting married, she would like her honeymoon on his lake. As he was saying good-bye, she told him she and Dan were looking forward to seeing him this coming weekend. He chuckled and then said he was happy they were still coming. After hanging up, Sue grabbed a book of practical jokes and found some that would be perfect if she could find her parents. *Okay, I just have to think like a detective and examine what I have so far: first clue. If they weren't in the area, they wouldn't have to keep it a secret. If they were in a cabin on a lake, they would be safe, because with all the lakes in Wisconsin, there would be no way I could narrow it down, so I think the water thing was just to throw me off. If they were at a motel nearby, that would still be pretty hard to find and break into. I've got it! I remember my dad showing Dan where they kept the spare key to their new house. I'm sure they thought I wasn't listening. That is where they*

*must be on their honeymoon. It makes sense; they are close by and figured I
would never think of them being right under my nose—that way they could
have another laugh.*

Sue planned to wait until Dan went to sleep and then head over to her
parents' house, but she fell asleep and didn't wake up until 2:00 a.m. She
got up and grabbed her bag of tricks and left. She talked to her car and
told it to start up without a sound and purr quietly down the driveway and
onto the road. The car must have listened, because she waited a minute
after getting to the road, and no light went on. She figured she was safe.
She got to her parents' house, and it was all dark. She parked on the street
and stopped and checked for mail or a newspaper, but there was neither.
She headed to the garage and looked in the window, and she saw only one
car. She went to the side door and picked up a white envelope taped to it,
which held the spare key. Just then there were bright lights in the driveway
and she thought, *Well, I caught them coming home.* But then some red
and blue lights came on, and she discovered it wasn't her parents, but the
police. They told her they had been watching her snoop around, looking
in the garage and looking for a key. They checked her drivers license which
showed she didn't live here. "I can explain, officers," she said.

"Yes, and you will, down at the station. We were warned about a heavy
set woman with auburn colored hair, checking to see if people were home
so she could rob them. She could possibly be working with a gang."

"That isn't me; this is my parents' house."

On the way to the station, Sue kept trying to explain. They wanted to
know why she would visit her parents at two o'clock in the morning and
were looking forward to her complete explanation, including why she had
latex gloves, a screw driver, hammer, knife, crackers, balloons, limburger
cheese, crayons and marshmallows in her car.

Sue prayed all the way to the station for God to bail her out. *After
all my work so this baby can have a nice respectable, stable home and family,
I can't ruin it by having him in jail and giving him a mom with a police
record.* There was no action at the police station, so they all wanted to
know if she was really pregnant, and regardless what would she be doing
snooping in windows at 2:00 a.m. First she told them about Dan and her
becoming Christians. As one officer got up to get coffee, he asked if what
she was doing was a religious thing. Another one added that maybe she
was like a Robin Hood—stealing from the rich to give to the poor. Sue
continued explaining about her parents, her matchmaking, and how she

had gone to the wedding thinking it was the wedding of a young couple but it had turned out to be her parents. That must have sounded a little fishy, because one of the officers asked if she had an invitation or if she just crashes weddings regularly. She told him she'd received the invitation but there was no name on it.

"Lady, I think you are digging your hole deeper and deeper. You received an invitation with no name on it. You went anyway, and it just happened to be your parents getting married, who you mentioned were barely speaking to each other."

The officers glanced at each other with looks that said "We have a real nutcase on our hands."

"What does all this have to do with you being at this house tonight? If you are an unwed mother, you don't have to go out and steal. We have agencies that will give you food and shelter, but now it looks like we will be providing that for you."

Sue told them there was more to this story, and they were very interested to hear it. They looked very skeptical when she told them that it was her parents' house that they had bought so they could live close by. "Then they went on their honeymoon and wouldn't tell me where because they don't trust me."

"Lady, you want us to trust you when your own parents don't?"

"Please, let me finish. I was only trying to find them to pay them back for not telling me anything."

"Your story has too many inconsistencies in it and does not make sense to any of us."

Just then the phone rang with the report on the house. "Ma'am, the house you were at tonight belongs to a couple in their thirties. These are you parents? How old are you?

"Yes, my parents are older, but they just bought this house from a couple in their thirties."

"Give us your parents' names and phone numbers, and we will check it out."

"Okay, but you will find out I am telling the truth. While you do that, do I get to make one phone call?"

"Yes, there is the phone."

Sue picked up the receiver thinking, *what am I going to say to my husband? He has never had a temper, but then I have never called him from jail.*

"Hello?"

"Hi, dear, don't panic; the baby and I are fine. I am just down at the police station and need you to come down and verify my story and get me out of here."

"You're what? I must be dreaming. Let me go check if you are in bed . . . . You're not there; where are you?"

"In jail; please come right away before they book me."

"Okay, I am on my way."

When Dan walked in he showed them his identification. They told him the charges were trespassing and attempted robbery. "She had many strange items in her possession which are suspect," said the desk attendant, "and a flashlight, which could be considered a weapon." Dan asked where they had picked her up and tried to verify to them that it really was her parents' address. "We need the truth, or you may be arrested as an accomplice. We checked, and that house belongs to a couple in their thirties. We called the numbers she gave us for her parents, and they are both disconnected. Sir, you are looking more and more like one of her gang members."

"Gang members? She doesn't have a gang."

"So you are admitting she works alone?"

"No, that is not what I meant."

They took Dan in another room to get his story, so they could compare. Sue could hear the conversation from her room. Dan started with the story of how they had received Jesus.

"Is this some kind of cult that likes to rob people?" said an officer. "You even send out pregnant women to do the stealing, hoping no one will arrest them."

Dan continued to explain. When he finished, he told them how long they had been at the same address, and that he had worked for the same company since high school. He then asked them if they had ever watched the television show *I Love Lucy*. They nodded. He said, "I think I am married to her twin. Lucy was taken to the police station for using counterfeit money and for taking change out of a till. In the same way, even though this situation looks bad, it isn't."

They found out he was telling the truth about his home and job, so they let him and Sue go home with orders not to leave town. Their last words were "Your stories better prove true, or you will be put in jail to await trial."

\*　　\*　　\*

Neither said a word all the way home. They went right to bed, and Dan felt like he had just gone to sleep when the alarm began going off. He staggered around to get ready for work while Sue lay there sound asleep. It was good she didn't wake up, because Dan was plenty mad, and the fact that she could still sleep made him even madder.

During break, Dan updated Stan on the latest developments and told him he needed prayer before he could go home to 'That Woman.' "Can you imagine getting woken up in the middle of the night and finding out your darling, sweet, gentle wife is in jail?" Dan said. "The worst was that by telling the truth, I ended up looking just as guilty as her."

At lunchtime, Stan and Dan grabbed their Bibles and sat down with their usual seekers and tormenters joining them. Nothing seemed like fun to Dan. Every verse Stan read was penetrating him like a bullet.

"Proverbs 15:1," said Stan, 'a soft answer turneth away wrath: but grievous words stir up anger.' It takes two to have a fight, and when one starts, the other instinctively fights back and it explodes. But a soft answer can stop all of that and produce peace instead of stress. This teaches how relevant the word of God is in this day and age, because if there is one thing there is plenty of in this world that is stress."

When Dan left work, Stan's final words were "Be ye kind."

"Right, and I will be able to give you a good report tomorrow," said Dan. He prayed in the Spirit, and by the time he pulled into his driveway, he was feeling the peace of God toward his wife. *Hopefully supper isn't ready yet, because somehow I have to make a call to Jake so he can inform my in-laws to call the police and verify our story. Otherwise, we can't leave town and go see them on Saturday. After they hear what their daughter did, they may not want to see her and might just leave before we get there.*

Dan walked in, and Sue had such a sad and sheepish look on her face that instead of being angry, he reminded himself how much he loved her, gave her a big hug, and said to her, "Everything will work out."

"You mean you're not mad at me?"

"I was extremely upset, but the word of God straightened me out. We will get through this together, and if you go to prison, I will go with you."

"What! We can't go to prison; we are going to have a baby, and he has a room right here."

"Calm down; everything will be fine. I am sure the police will recheck everything and find out you were telling the truth."

"Yes, but if they don't, we can't go see Jake this weekend."

"I will work on it. I will be in the den; just call me when supper is ready."

Dan quickly and quietly closed the door and called Jake, who informed him that his in-laws had gone into town for supper. "I have a message for them; I have to make it brief and will explain on Saturday. Sue got caught by the police snooping around their house, and they need to call and verify that it is their house and Sue is their daughter and she has permission to be there."

"Wow! I will give them the message, and I definitely look forward to the rest of the story."

Just as Dan hung up, Sue called him for supper. Afterward, they had a Bible study and time of prayer to vacuum their minds.

Each day, Sue stared at the phone thinking the police would call any minute to tell her they had verified her story and closed the case. It took until Friday morning for the call to come. When Dan came home, Sue ran—or rather waddled—out to tell him the good news. He was nonchalant about it, as if he knew what the outcome would be all along.

# Chapter Twenty-Five

On Saturday morning, Dan and Sue were up bright and early and headed out to Jake's. The sky was bursting with an array of blues that was hard for them to look away from. The country roads and the many cornfields looked like a painting for them to enjoy. They talked of nice juicy corn on the cob dipped in butter. At the same time, they both spotted a rainbow, which seemed to signal new beginnings. The previous few days had been so great and so awful all in one. There wasn't much said between them, but each sensed the other was thinking the same thing.

Jake was very happy to see them, and their room was fixed up so nice that it almost looked like a honeymoon suite. He had a lot to tell them, but he had prepared a big brunch, so they needed to eat first. As soon as they had unpacked, they went into the kitchen and noticed there were five place settings. Sue asked, "Jake, are more people joining us?"

She was thinking, *how wonderful! Jake is getting more and more social. I really didn't want to share him, mainly because we came to hear every detail of the visit from his children, but I will keep my mouth shut in front of strangers and will be patient and wait.*

Just then there was a knock on the door, and Jake went to answer it. He came back and announced, "Let me present the newlyweds to you: Mr. and Mrs. Mom and Dad."

Sue's jaw dropped, but she quickly closed her mouth and asked, "What are you doing here?"

"We are on our honeymoon and should ask the same question. What are you doing here? Aren't you supposed to be in jail? Is there no justice? Or did you escape and we have a fugitive on our hands?"

"That means you must know everything."

"Juicy gossip like that cannot be contained. I know that as Christians we are not supposed to do that, but as parents, we need to know when our children go astray so we can help them back on the right path. We will continue to work on that, but for now let's eat before the food gets cold."

\*   \*   \*

After lunch Sue made the announcement that it felt like the baby could come any day.

For the rest of the day, the family didn't pick on Sue, and she tried to keep her mouth shut and just blend in to avoid being the topic of conversation.

They all went to Jake's church the next morning. "I hope it isn't another sermon directed at me," Sue whispered to Dan. When the pastor announced it was titled "How Great Is Our God?" Sue let out a sigh of relief. The pastor explained that the Bible is coded and until a person is born again they don't see and understand just how wonderful God is.

In the afternoon Dan and Sue headed home with lots of events to talk about. They walked into the house, and Dan realized that as much fun as traveling was, there was no place like home sweet home. He thought it was especially nice to be here and not visiting his wife in jail."

\*   \*   \*

As Sue's due date approached, she began doing less work and more sitting and reading her Bible. She read the Ten Commandments to her unborn baby over and over again. She once said to Dan, "God expects a lot, even out of children; so like Samuel, they have to be encouraged to wait on the Lord and hear his voice and obey."

Even if Sue could have done more work, she would not have had time because of all the phone calls. She passed her due date, and Dan began coming home during his lunch breaks. Between her mom and her mother-in-law stopping in or calling, she couldn't get much rest.

One Saturday morning, while lying in bed, Sue was thinking, *this should be the day. Dan is home, my suitcase is packed, and even though I love being pregnant, I am done.* All of a sudden she felt something strange. She thought maybe it was a contraction, but she knew it could have just been gas. She waited and waited, and just when she had decided it was nothing, it came again. She grabbed her watch and thought; *I am going to be timing either gas pains or contractions. Maybe I ate something that doesn't agree with me. There are just too many possibilities. But if this is the baby, I don't want to wait too long. I don't think Dan would like to have to do the delivering.*

She lay there thinking, *what is wrong with me Lord? Isn't a woman supposed to know when her baby is coming?* Just then another contraction came, and she was pretty sure—more like positive—that it was the real thing. After she was dressed, she woke Dan up, saying, "It's time to go."

"Okay, I know exactly what to do."

Dan got up and grabbed the suitcase and walked out the door. Sue heard him start the car. *I hope he isn't going without me and in his pajamas. What would he say once he got to the hospital? That could be interesting. "Um, my wife is having a baby, but I forgot to bring her."* He must have come to his senses, because he came back in the house looking very sheepish. "I will be ready in a minute," he said. Are you all right?"

"Yes I am, but what about you?"

"I'm fine, but when you woke me up, I just automatically kicked into 'get to the hospital and hurry' mode. I guess I forget we have to do this together."

On their way to the hospital, the contractions began getting closer and stronger, and Sue did some mild screaming. Dan pulled up to the hospital door and jumped out and ran inside. He started yelling, "My baby is coming; my baby is coming!" The receptionist inquired about his wife, and it dawned on him that he had left Sue in the car. Dan ran back out and picked her up and said that they needed her in there.

As they wheeled Sue away, she was hoping Dan would remember things like their names and addresses so he could fill out the paperwork. Sue told the baby he couldn't come until his dad got there. When Dan arrived in the birthing room, Sue was one big push away from bringing Benjamin Daniel into the world. When he was cleaned up, they gave him to Dan first in hopes of calming him down, and it worked, except for the tears coming down Dan's eyes and getting his son all wet. Dan and Sue looked at each other and then at their son and said at the same time, "Our miracle baby."

After Sue and Benjamin were settled, Dan looked at his wife and sighed, "It sure was hard work having a baby." Zzzzzzzzzzz

CPSIA information can be obtained at www.ICGtesting.com
Printed in the USA
LVOW081206240912

300063LV00001B/2/P